The Baker and The Billionaire

by

Lina Gardiner

The Baker and The Billionaire

Cover Art by *Lisa Dawn MacDonald*

The Wild Rose Press, Inc.
PO Box 708
Adams Basin, NY 14410-0708
Visit us at www.thewildrosepress.com

Publishing History
First Edition, 2025
Trade Paperback ISBN 978-1-5092-6115-4
Digital ISBN 978-1-5092-6114-7

Published in the United States of America

Dedication

To Kate Kelly, my wonderful friend and author who lost her life to breast cancer. Always in my heart.

Chapter One

Cole Prentice watched as a blonde knockout, with striking violet eyes, entered his penthouse office. Even though the sway of her hips made his mouth go dry, he held back a grin when she stared him down with a determined expression that begged him to show her who was boss.

Instead, he inhaled, straightened his shoulders, then put his pen down before he snapped it in two. "I'm guessing you're Ms. Cameron?" he managed in a dry, disinterested voice.

Her lips pursed, and her eyes narrowed on him, just a little.

Not what he expected—by her reaction, he guessed she didn't want to be here anymore than he wanted her here. Not so much shocked by her reaction as intrigued by it, he admitted she wasn't what he'd expected. Most women pictured dollar signs when they met him. He'd long since given up hope of finding a true mate.

He bit his lip. Whomever the matchmaking company sent they should be a willing participant, someone who wanted this, right? And yet, he'd bet a million dollars this woman didn't like him—and didn't mind letting him know.

Was this the matchmaker's tactic to reel in the biggest fish? If so, the concept appealed. The last thing he wanted was a gold digger hanging on his every word. He sighed. He didn't have time for this right now, but his board of directors expected him to produce a fiancée or wife within a short timeframe. With no one suitable, and with no desire to find a wife, Cole hired Rosa, matchmaker to the wealthy, to soften his media profile.

Examining the uninterested Ms. Cameron standing in front of him, he had to admit Rosa had hit a home run in the visual department. Ms. Cameron was stunning, if a little tense and angry. She had a bod few women carried without great genes. Her eyes were striking, a clear blue-violet, but he couldn't decide which. Her cheekbones would be the envy of most women he knew. He chastised himself. It wasn't her cheekbones that drew his attention. "Have a seat." He hoped his monotone voice would tick her off to give him a chance to even out his unwanted thoughts.

She sat and crossed her long legs in one smooth motion.

Her actions made his mouth go dry. Words faltered. "So…" Why would this woman need a matchmaker? He tapped a fingernail against his mahogany desk while many distasteful reasons sprang to mind—number one, his money. He had no choice. If things continued to his plan, she'd take some attention away from areas of his life which were best forgotten.

"Mr. Prentice?" She tapped her watch.

"Yes, let's get down to business." He bit back a knowing grin. Few people would have noticed her irritation because she'd masked her feelings well, but he'd learned to go a level deeper. He had a talent for reading people. That was how he became suspicious about two Information Technology employees who'd set up a shadow account to skim funds from his company. "Is there anything you'd like to know about me?" He seated himself on the front of his desk and leaned just enough to be in her personal space. Not so close as to make her uncomfortable, but close enough to show her he was the boss in this office.

"I've read the Boston papers, and I've got the gist of things." She brushed a piece of lint off her sleeve.

Slam! He leaned back and pursed his lips before nodding. "Well, I'm sure you know newspapers and magazines have a tendency to sensationalize the truth about people." Her vibrant violet eyes riveted on him, not in the least affected by his cool treatment.

"In what way?" she asked.

She was good! But not so good he couldn't handle her, and a dozen more, just like her. With an impatient glance at his own watch, he ignored her question. "Taking time to get to know you would have been better before we ended up at the wrong end of a journalist's camera, but..."

"But it's not so easy when you hire Rosa at the last minute, and you need a date right away." She stared at her hands.

She'd nailed that statement. And she wasn't afraid to speak the truth. Unable to sit still a minute longer, he strode to the window and gazed out. "I understand you've been briefed about tonight. I scheduled an appointment for you to buy a new gown for the formal function." He adjusted his cuff. "My limo is waiting downstairs. The chauffeur will wait until you find your dress, after which he'll take you home to get ready." He glanced over his shoulder.

"I beg your pardon?" She shifted forward stiffly in

her seat.

"He'll pick you up again at seven forty-five p.m." He snagged a card from his pocket and handed her the chauffeur's phone number. "Just call him when you're ready, but please be prompt. I expect to be at the charity auction at eight fifteen."

She bit her lip. "You're not going out to dinner with me? To get to know me?"

Her question surprised him. He'd have thought she'd be happy to dine alone. He shook his head. "I don't have time, but if you'd like to have dinner first, just ask my chauffeur to drop you off at a restaurant. Have whatever you want on my dime. Just finish on time to meet me."

Exhaling, she shook her head. "Don't you want to know anything about me first?"

No doubt she realized he was a jerk for expecting her to go to dinner by herself. And, to prove that point, every time he opened his mouth to speak, he noted irritation spiked in her expression. He held up his hands. "Unnecessary." He'd hoped not to irritate her to where she'd leave him high and dry.

With a exaggerated exhalation, she frowned in his direction, then at his desk.

His gaze shifted to the papers on his desk. "I guess it's fair, since you got your information about me from an outside source, that I did the same." He tidied the sheets. Anger flicked behind those gorgeous violet eyes, and Cole wondered why. Her biography had been pristine—had he missed something?

"My answers were private—for Rosa's information." She gripped the arm of her chair to stop from leaving right now.

"Given my inability to buy a cup of coffee without making waves, I had to be sure you'd survive a date with me." He used a tentative pause to full effect.

"I see." She tipped her head just enough to prove her disinterest. "You had to know if any skeletons would pop out of my closet." Her pretty eyes narrowed for a second.

His gaze slid to her glistening lips for a beat too long. He'd better stop there. Assessing her any further might get his face slapped. Not that he wouldn't deserve it. And, besides, she was the last thing he needed right now. "I'll see you tonight." He returned to his desk again and picked up a pen. He expected her to take the cue and leave.

"Let me get this straight." Her eyes narrowed. "You're assuming I don't already have a dress suitable for your function and I have to go buy one?"

"I don't want to insult you, of course. In my experience, most women would jump at buying a new dress when they don't have to pay for it. And given the caliber of the event, the coordinators have a certain expectation about how we must dress for this function." He forced a smile.

She huffed out a quick breath. "I don't take gifts from men I don't know."

He digested her statement for a moment. "It'll be a thank-you for agreeing to come with me tonight, Kate." He'd swear she was about to tell him where to go before her expression changed and she masked her feelings again.

"I'll go along with this on one condition." She stood and faced him at his desk.

"Your condition?"

"I choose the dress. I'm not wearing something a brainless bimbo would wear to date an egocentric billionaire."

Both brows rose. "I should hope not." Put in his place again. She would not be used. He hoped she understood who she was dealing with. Not some inexperienced boy who didn't know how to handle her, if he wished. Good thing he didn't have time for games—not even pleasurable ones. "Since I'm too busy to go and pick it out myself, I'll leave the choice up to you." He took his time, monitoring every inch of her outfit. "It's obvious you dress in a tasteful manner. I'm sure you won't disappoint."

A slow flush worked its way up her neck.

His insides hardened like cement. Why was he doing this? He wasn't in the market for a relationship, nor marriage. That said, Kate had more guts than most of the men who entered this office. He liked that. Too bad she believed everything she read in the papers; he could see it in her eyes.

With a stiff back, she strode out of his office.

Left gaping after her, he bit the end of his pen and considered what might happen if he'd been serious when he hired Rosa, The Matchmaker. Would this woman have been his match? He'd never know, because she was just a hired date and nothing else.

Cole returned his attention to the paperwork on his desk, shuffled a few pages, then quit. He couldn't get his mind off the blonde sophisticate who'd just left his office.

A quick rap on the door sounded, and Josh Jones entered. Josh stood six inches shorter and a little rounder in the middle than Cole, but he stood tall in the boardroom. He was an ace at dealing with people.

As the top executive in the firm and trusted friend, Josh had been savvy to Cole's plans to save the firm. And, he was aware about what Cole's father had done to the company. He was also aware how hard Cole had to work to rebuild the funds for the sake of his employees and their pensions.

"So, boss, how'd it go with the…?" Josh sat in the same seat Kate had been in moments before.

"You talking about the two employees caught with their virtual fingers in the till?"

"Nah. I trusted you to handle them without a problem."

Pressing a hand over his mouth, Cole grimaced. "Not something I needed right now, though."

"No. I agree." Josh leaned forward and allowed a boyish grin. "What about the woman?"

Cole hesitated. Not used to being candid about his personal life, he admitted Josh was someone he could trust. "Not bad. I don't think she'll run away scared, if that's what you mean. She seems to have spunk."

Josh grinned. "Rosa is amazing at finding the right match. She doesn't get it wrong when she sets people up."

Thinking hard about that, Cole frowned. "Easy for you to say. You have Janna. You didn't need a matchmaker to find someone for you."

Josh's face flushed, and his mouth twitched.

Cole's eyebrows shot up. "Wait. Are you saying Rosa found Janna and you never told me?"

"How else can a working man who's got life-shattering long hours find the right woman?" Josh grinned in a sly manner.

"I notice you take all your vacations now." Cole hid a grin.

"Damn straight. I'm crazy in love. I want to spend every minute with Janna, even after being married for two whole years."

Something shifted in Cole's chest. Not jealousy. Not regret. He had the job he wanted. He'd been groomed for this lifestyle. Why should he care about being married to a woman who loved him for himself?

Chapter Two

Perched on a chair in the boutique dressing room, Kate dug the cell phone out of her purse and poked in the number. The phone rang at the other end four times before Rosa answered.

"I didn't think you would answer the phone."

"Course I would, sweetie. I was just busy."

A hint of guilt blossomed in her friend's voice. "My eyeball! You were afraid I planned to quit on you."

"You're not phoning to quit, are you? How'd the introductions go?"

Kate let out an exasperated sigh. "As suspected. He's more than a little arrogant, and bossy, and...he sent me to VanBuren's in order to find a *suitable* dress for tonight—on his tab. And, right now, I feel like the hooker in *Pretty Woman*."

"Except you could shop there on your own dime, if you were so inclined," Rosa said.

"I'm not inclined to waste my hard-earned wages. She gaped at the price tag. "On a twenty-thousand-dollar dress!" She and Rosa had very different ideas about spending money.

"Oh, honey, you're shopping in the bargain basement, aren't you? Prentice would want you to have the most up-to-date style for his function. Go back upstairs and get something new and designer. He will prefer a one-of-a-kind dress. You'll have to trust me on this."

Kate chewed her lip. "I can't believe I'm doing this. What if he finds out I'm not one of your typical millionaire recruits? Not to mention, I have an abnormal dislike of rich, powerful men and a bad history with the media."

"Oh, honey, that's not true," Rosa said.

"Wish I could agree, but I've seen that life and just managed to get out in one piece. Unscathed is not in my vernacular."

"You've got to put that idiot behind you. Consider what you've accomplished all by yourself. It took strength to manage after your fiancé left you holding the check."

Heat built behind her eyes. "Not by myself. I had help from a very generous friend. I'd have gone bankrupt without you, Rosa."

"Ahhh, that doesn't count. That was just a little leg up." Rosa cleared her throat. "So, sweetie, what was your first impression of the man in question, aside from the fact he is everything you want to avoid?"

With the phone against her ear, Kate left the changing room and took the stairs up to the next floor while they talked. She understood what Rosa meant. Rosa always believed first impressions were of extreme importance, and she had keen intuition based on those first impressions. If Kate played her cards right, then Rosa could pick an appropriate match for the billionaire in question, and Kate could back out without creating a fuss.

"You know—rich jerk. Thinks he can show off by buying a...forty thousand dollar dress!" She grasped her throat. "For one night."

"Thank God, you've gone upstairs. I can tell you are checking price tags by the way you're gasping." Rosa laughed. "Either that or you didn't take the elevator and you're out of shape."

"Out of shape? No way. I go to the gym three nights a week." Whereas Rosa hated the gym with a passion and remained slim with little to no exertion, Kate had to work at maintaining her preferred weight. She sighed again.

"Some people just don't know how to spend their spare time." Rosa's humor carried in her voice.

"I guess," Kate whispered. "Listen, I'd better go spend wild money to show off the arrogant billionaire." She might wear the outfit tonight, but she'd return the dress by courier first thing in the morning. He could donate it to the Salvation Army for all she cared. She would never keep such an expensive gift from a stranger.

"You have to make sure you get one that shows great cleavage."

"Rosa!"

"What? You know how important cleavage is…"

Kate looked at the ceiling and inhaled a long breath.

"Hold it. Hold it. You didn't describe your first impression of him. I will not let you get away until you tell me."

"I could just hang up." Kate loved to tease Rosa.

"But you won't do that to your best friend…"

"He's overconfident." She shook her head against her better judgement. "But something in his eyes belies everything I've read." She had to be honest, as much as she wanted to run him into the ground. "It's like he's more than meets the eye. Just not sure if it's a good or a bad thing. You know I've never been as good at first impressions as you."

Rosa giggled.

"What? What does it mean?"

"Nothing, sweetie. It means this ordeal will not be as hard as you expected. Maybe his whole arrogant role is just a part of his marketing?"

"What kind of idiot would market himself that way?"

"A smart one, maybe? Think about how that horror author markets himself as a scary, crazed individual."

"Which maybe he is? Why do I feel like I've just fallen down the rabbit hole?"

"Because you swallowed the potion that made you so tall." Rosa laughed at her own joke.

Rosa was a petite woman at about five foot-two in stature, but in personality she stood as tall as any person Kate had ever met. She drew people in and became instant friends with those she deemed worth the effort.

"You're so funny, Rosa. Hilarious." Someone poked Kate in the arm, and she twisted with the phone still at her ear.

"Can I help you, Miss?" A gaunt woman with frizzy hair that appeared as dry as straw glared down her long nose.

Could it be, because Kate wore off-the-rack clothes and rifling through the designer dresses while talking on the phone? "I'd like to see some of your evening gowns." Kate forced a stern look. "Designer gowns— one-of-a-kind gowns, please." Kate spoke loud enough for Rosa to hear her. At least she got some satisfaction when she requested the most expensive gowns in the shop, that wiped the smug smirk off the clerk's face. "Gotta go, Rosa. Frivolous money to spend."

Rosa laughed in the background while she clicked off.

Once she found the gown, the fabric slid over her skin like heaven the minute she put it on. Dark red silk taffeta and low cut, the bodice hugged her shape, and soft folds flared out to the floor. And, long enough that the dress swept to the floor. Bonus!

"Don't tell me the price." She held up a hand to block the terrifying cost on the price tag. Maybe, if she didn't know how much it cost, she might wear the amazing gown without too much panic. The garment did astonishing things to her figure and should knock Mr. Cole Prentice onto his holier-than-thou rump. "Just wrap it up and put it on Cole Prentice's tab." She'd never had to try not to sound like a kept woman.

"As soon as I verify that with Mr. Prentice."

The woman's condescending, nasal voice made Kate grind her teeth together. She was about to shove the dress at the woman and tell her to put it back.

Another lady rushed up. "Excuse me, Madam, I'm Marcia, the manager. Please let me help you." The manager waved the condescending salesperson away. "It's not a problem, ma'am. Mr. Prentice called while you were in the changing room and said to show you every courtesy. I'll handle your sale."

"Thank you." Kate forced herself to sound polite while fighting the urge to put the gown back and tell Rosa she couldn't do it. Rosa needed her, though. Kate owed her. If she was playing a part, she had to be believable everywhere, including a designer dress shop.

One small slip-up and the game would be over.

And worse, for Rosa.

****

That evening, Cole stepped out of the shower, dried off, and dressed in his best black silk tux. He took stock in the full-length mirror, adjusted his thick brown hair a little on the right side, then ruffled it back again. Why was he paying more attention than normal to his appearance? It couldn't be for the haughty woman who'd agreed to be his date tonight.

She was tall for a woman, at least five foot ten, a complementary height to his six foot four frame. Her blonde hair appeared natural. She had a bod any man would notice and without plastic surgery enhancements, as far as he could tell. A pleasant change. Most of the women in his circle of friends were rather plastic and too doll-like for his tastes.

Her eyes were a soft violet, very unusual. He'd already noted they'd changed color when he irritated her. A grin surfaced at that information. He enjoyed a challenge, and she'd be just that.

"Cole, the limo's here," Victoria Prentice shouted from the lower level.

He'd almost forgotten his mother was still here. She'd stopped in to use his gym. As of late, she'd been on a body-building kick. "Give your voice a break, Mom, use the intercom," Cole said to himself and grinned. Victoria Prentice could hobnob with the best of them, but deep down, she was a good-ole girl from West Virginia. He loved that about his mother.

He finished tying his bowtie, grabbed his wallet and shoved it into his jacket pocket, then ran down the stairs, ignoring the beaming smile greeting him from the bottom step.

"You're gorgeous, dear. So what's up? Don't tell me you have a date?"

She'd know more than she wanted to soon enough, because the paparazzi would splash it all over the papers by tomorrow. And none of it would be true. "Going on a date is no big deal, Mom."

"Of course it's a big deal. Not to mention you could use a little relaxation. You appear tired."

Cole hoped his mother didn't notice the stiffness in his posture. She was right. He needed a break. He'd been tired of it all. But he was, at least, at the point where he could soon relax just a little.

"Will she be coming inside? Or are you picking her up?" Victoria asked.

Cole adjusted his shirt sleeves and rotated his shoulders to find a comfort zone. "Jason, the chauffeur, is picking her up."

"Oh, honey, that's not any way to treat a date."

"She is just escorting me to tonight's function. Not worth bringing her home to meet you."

"Why not? I'd love to meet her." Victoria smiled when she picked up a photo he'd taken of her last Christmas.

"This is our first date, Mother. We wouldn't want to scare her away." He kissed her forehead.

Victoria laughed.

Her salt-and-pepper black hair, always coiffed, accentuated her high cheekbones. Dressed in designer workout clothes that showed off her trim figure, he sometimes forgot she was fifty-five. She'd been divorced from Cole's father for eight years, and he wished she could find a nice man. Come to think of it, maybe that's why she was interested in the gym. Had she found someone?

"I wouldn't dream of scaring her away." Victoria sounded a little miffed.

No, he'd do that all by himself. No sense getting his mother's hopes up by taking home a rent-a-girlfriend. Not that Rosa's matchmaking company supplied such services. "Maybe you can meet her some other time." He watched his mother pull a face because she, of all people, understood that meant—not likely. "Love you."

"Don't forget, Cole. I want to meet her." Victoria patted his shoulder.

"Good night, Mother." He winked.

The limo waited. He cracked the door and leaned in to enter. A mere glance in Kate's direction caused him to halt his breathing. She'd been graceful in his office, but she was beyond beautiful in the back of his limo with a low-cut red gown that made her sexy as hell, and she smelled just as wonderful. "Good evening." He looked her over. "Nice dress." That's all he dared to say. At this point, to stare wouldn't be good because she disliked him to start with.

While his practiced self-control kicked in, he wasn't used to having to check his breathing in the presence of a beautiful woman. Most often, he was disappointed rather than excited, because he'd been jaded by what women wanted. At least this one was different. She wasn't feigning her lack of interest, he'd bet his wallet on it.

"Thank you."

She kept any hint of emotion from her voice in that statement. In fact, her serious expression helped tamp down his first reaction to her image in that dress. Good thing he was an expert at maintaining an outward cool demeanor. "Have you had dinner?"

She gazed out her window. "Not on your dime. I ate at home before your chauffeur picked me up."

Good thing she wasn't paying attention to his wide grin, because she'd think he was making fun of her statement. Instead, he believed her. She wasn't pretending she didn't want him to throw money at her. How unusual. "Tell me, did you pick the dress out yourself? Or did the manager pick it out?"

Her head whipped around, and she frowned. "I don't need someone else to pick my clothes out. I can do it on my own, although I object to you buying such an expensive dress for one night. It's not something I'd allow in any other situation."

Again, the grin beckoned, but given the way she was eyeing him right now, he didn't dare let it show. "I understand, and I appreciate you did buy the dress as requested. The media will scrutinize you tonight, but while I'm sure you can buy your own dresses, I'm sending a message to the media to indicate you are a serious girlfriend. The media will know everything about your gown before they release the papers in the morning. Consider this a little of marketing and a thank-you for going along with my plan."

She frowned straight ahead. "Will they also know I am returning it in the morning, too? Because I am."

Idiot. He was most often suave in situations like this. Why was he acting like a tongue-tied teenager? Not that he didn't have the desire to lick his way from those luscious lips down to the magnificent cleavage on display. He forced his gaze away and stared out his window in order to maintain dignity.

"Considering you paid forty thousand dollars for this dress, good thing you at least approve."

Even though the words *hell yeah*! danced on his tongue, he managed a dry tone. "It's fine." His response had come out more clipped than he had meant, and he could again see fire erupt behind her gaze.

As an eligible bachelor, he'd dated beautiful women. The truth being, most had been a disappointment and hadn't gotten past the first date. Nevertheless, the media had been cruel and wrong when they'd speculated about his love life. The rags had hinted at his string of one-night stands and called him the frozen king.

"Don't worry. I can pretend we have an amicable relationship when we get to the event." Her voice mimicked his earlier monotone.

A dig. And, yes, he'd deserved it. He glanced at her again, wondering about the subtle scent she wore. She'd done her hair up with a few soft curls accenting her face. He'd liked it down, swirling around her shoulders, but this style appeared more sophisticated. She could be a model. She had the lines for it. Given that, she avoided eye contact. Maybe he'd been wrong? Maybe this evening would be an epic disaster.

The limo approached the red carpet.

On an impulse, he touched her hand resting on the leather seat between them to put her at ease. Was it to put her at ease, or him?

She jerked her hand away. When her gaze met his, she smiled, but it didn't reach her eyes. "Sorry to be jumpy. I can do this. We'll get through it. You don't have to worry."

"Good." *What had she meant by that?*

Chapter Three

Outside the Gala, Kate waited for Cole to climb out of the limo before she slid toward the door. Panic fluttered out of control in her chest when she spotted the photographers. She'd be in the media's spotlight, but that didn't mean she wouldn't hate it. The second she stood and Cole stretched out a hand, flashbulbs blinded her. She blinked to get the spots out of her vision.

Cole created a buzz wherever he travelled, and he projected an uptight version of James Bond in that tux. His mouth, often pinched and serious, had a sensual appeal for the cameras in the shadows. He was a talented actor. She'd have to remember that.

A warm hand on her back sent the message to start down the red carpet. Not a problem. The faster she got out of here, the better. *He would be as capable of holding a woman in his arms as juggling a dozen companies.* Confusing to think like that.

How could she risk the media dredging up all the old lies? Her steps faltered, and she wanted to run.

As if he knew what she'd been thinking, his hand took hers and squeezed, smiling to de-escalate her fear. His lips brushed her ear in a faux intimate gesture.

"I know this is a challenge, but we can fake it, can't we?" he whispered.

Somehow, this whole thing enacted terrible

memories of her ex-fiancé and how the media had treated her then. This was a big mistake. How had she let Rosa talk her into it? She glanced back at the limo already driving away from the curb.

"Please." He met her gaze.

She noted his smile had reached his eyes.

"The last thing I need is more bad publicity tonight."

Okay, so he didn't care that she had feelings. Maybe he wasn't the most sensitive of billionaires. What had she expected from someone like him? She sucked in a quick breath and prayed the press would be gentle this time because she'd been at their mercy before. If her last relationship gone wrong was released again, Cole might not be thrilled with Rosa's matchmaking. The whole thing could blow up in their faces.

But, of course, Cole must have researched her background. Unless Rosa had given him a whitewashed version. Either way, he'd have had her checked out—it wouldn't surprise her if he'd been apprised of every dirty little secret Rodney Hollander had told the press—all of them lies. And yet, why the continued charade?

She'd lived the sting of tabloid reporters' nasty, untrue stories. Rodney had fueled most of them to improve his own image. Maybe Rosa imagined the rumors would make her more sympathetic to Cole's situation. His expression appeared pinched, even though he smiled.

She stiffened her spine and sucked in a long breath. As long as Prentice didn't humiliate her, and then feed her to the sharks, she could manage. She'd come to terms with having her life dissected in public, hadn't she? Never mind that she'd promised Rosa she could do this. Having the media focus on her bakery rather than her this time would be nice. That kind of PR would be helpful.

His smile was genuine, albeit showing slight relief when her tension lessened, and she met his gaze, then nodded. They continued down the red carpet, her hand clasped in his warm, strong fingers.

According to the media, this fund-raiser was a pet project of Cole's. Kate was his paid-for arm-candy. She could pretend for the short time she needed to, even though somewhere deep inside, she had the feeling this whole thing was going south, fast.

Inside the massive banquet hall, she scanned her surroundings. Thick red carpeting helped with acoustics, and gold chandeliers added to the rich feel of the room. Round dining tables were set with crystal glasses, silver cutlery, and gold nametags at each plate. The $1000-a-plate fund-raiser consisted, to the largest percent, of businesspeople. While some causes were near-and-dear to her own heart, this venue wouldn't be one she could afford.

Lost in her problems, she'd almost missed a cue when Cole tried to keep her in the conversation with a couple of men she'd recognized from the papers. This fund-raiser included at least ten different groups vying for money to help the poor and the disadvantaged.

An hour later, she noted the tired expression behind Cole's eyes. He'd written a half dozen very generous checks. Did his generosity stem from real concern, or was it just a tax-break or a marketing ploy?

Kate stepped away to powder her nose. When she returned, Kate found Cole chatting with a man and two beautiful women whose perfect makeup made them look exotic. Their rapt attention was on Cole.

Why had he needed Rosa to find him a date? That he had his pick of the crop was clear. Or were these women more interested in his money than his reputation? Knowing if someone wanted him for himself or his money would be pretty much impossible. She suspected plenty of women would put up with his attitude in favor of his money, a powerful lure for some women.

Being a fantastic actor, he all but devoured her with his gaze.

Even though she recognized his expression as fake, she forced a sweet smile in his direction, the whole time telling herself she owed Rosa, and she had to find out what Cole Prentice needed in a woman. This would only take a couple of days.

Meanwhile, he acted as if he had eyes for her alone.

She gritted her teeth. She stepped close and took his hand in hers. "Miss me?" she whispered and hoped she hadn't gone overboard.

"Darling, of course." He grinned, kissing her wrist before returning to the person he'd been speaking to. "Ah, I'm sorry. What was I saying?"

The man he was talking to winked. "I think I've kept you too long from your date."

Reminding herself that she had a job to do, she squeezed his hand. He circled her waist with one arm and settled his hand on her hip in a proprietary manner. His warm hand burned through the dress as if it left a brand on her skin. She had to fight the urge not to run. Feeling someone tap her shoulder, she took the opportunity to step away from Cole's embrace.

Seeing Brianne Sunhurst, an old university acquaintance approach, Kate's spirits flagged.

"Kate, what a surprise to see you here." Her gaze flicked to Cole.

"It's a surprise for me, too," Kate responded, then bit her tongue.

Cole slanted her a cool glance before smiling.

Had it been a warning? "Cole, this is my friend from school, Brianne Sunhurst." Had she been too obvious that she and Brianna were not friends?

"Hello, Mr. Prentice." She smiled, her full lips glistening under a thick layer of pink gloss.

Brianne made people feel special just with the tone of her voice, and people always fell for it.

"Nice to meet you, Brianne." Cole smiled, an honest smile this time. His face transformed.

Kate found herself transfixed but more ticked-off than she should be. He used Brianne's first name as if he'd known her forever. Why? Cole called her Ms. Cameron.

Cole asked Brianne several questions about her friendship with Kate.

No doubt, Brianne would think he was interested, but he was digging for more information on Kate.

Brianne chatted non-stop.

Kate tuned her out until Cole touched her elbow.

"Excuse me, darling, I have to speak to the director of the fundraiser, and he's coming this way."

Her breathing faltered at his use of the word darling. He was smooth. And it was easy to see Brianne believed it.

"You're so lucky to have snagged a man like him."

Her gaze remained glued to Cole's back.

"Thank you." No way would she say any more and give herself away.

"How's Rosa these days, Kate? I haven't run into her in ages. Are you two still doing the university girlfriend's weekend retreat every fall in the White Mountains? I'd love to go along with the group this year. It's been way too long since I've seen everyone."

Uh oh! That was the last thing she expected Brianne to say. Kate recognized Brianne's fake smile where some wouldn't. A flush whooshed across Kate's skin. She stole a furtive glance at Cole's back. He appeared to be listening to the event director. She had to hope he hadn't overheard Brianne, or she'd be in major soup. He was too smart not to catch on right away that she wasn't an actual client.

Brianne's cell phone began ringing, but before she answered it, she gave Kate a faux-peck on the cheek and handed her a business card. "Call me when you get a chance." Her gaze wandered to Cole again before she hurried off, as if she'd been expecting an important call.

"You and your friend caught up?" Cole asked as soon as the director left.

Kate bit her lip and nodded. Brianne was never a friend. She used people and threw them away. The only reason Brianne wanted to join Kate and Rosa for their annual get-together was because Kate appeared to be dating Cole Prentice, and Brianne wanted to get to know him better.

"Good." He kept his voice casual, then flicked his shirt cuff back to glance at his watch. "I think it's time we go, isn't it, darling?" His gaze caught hers, heat flaring at the same moment his hand ran across the bare skin on her back, then rested on her nape.

A shiver flashed down her spine. She covered her discomfort but wasn't doing a wonderful job.

He leaned down. "Please go with what I'm about to do," he whispered. He drew her toward him, then planted his lips on hers.

The kiss lasted longer than it should have in public. Kate should have stopped it, but she'd been too busy reacting to his mouth against hers. Melting against him, she closed her eyes and let her world spin. Cool air settled between them as he backed away. Her legs grew heavy, as if they couldn't budge.

But he covered it up by spinning her away from the flashing cameras and tucking her into the crook of his arm.

Fingers shaking, she touched her mouth to smooth her lipstick that had to be smudged.

"I'm sorry I surprised you," he whispered.

"I'm not your hired…" she began.

"I love to make her blush." He covered her words because too many people were within earshot.

Several people laughed.

Kate cringed. Her mantra, *this is for Rosa*, kept running over and over in her head.

"Can I get you a drink before we leave, my love? You appear a little flushed."

"No, thank you," she answered through clenched teeth.

He glanced at his watch again. "Good. It's time we go. We have other things on our agenda tonight, don't we?"

Burning with embarrassment, she dashed out of the party, lifting her gown with one hand so she wouldn't trip on the way down the stairs to the waiting limo.

The driver held the door open.

She dove inside with Cole following, camera lights flashing so often everything was a blurry scene of spots.

Even before the driver had left the curbside, Cole started undoing his tie, then the top two buttons of his shirt. "Sorry about the way I covered for your surprise in there."

She glared. He didn't appear all that sorry. In fact, he had an uncharacteristic expression of contentment on his face. "Why'd you do that? You don't even know me."

He grinned. "Had to. You didn't act like someone who was on a date with me."

His voice had held a stiff edge again. Back to arrogant billionaire mode. "I beg your pardon." Bile rose in her throat. "You send me off to buy a dress and have dinner on my own. You don't spend even a few minutes to get to know me. Yet, you expect me to melt and go with it when you manhandle me in public?"

Sighing, he cast a bland expression in her direction. "Yes, I really do, and that was a far cry from manhandling."

"If that's your idea of how this thing is supposed to work, I think you're confused. We're on a date, Cole. We're supposed to be getting to know each other to see if we're a match. I'm not your paid-for entertainment."

"You're also supposed to be a client picked from a vetted list, not Rosa's buddy. What the hell games are you two playing?"

His voice deepened into a soft growl when he got angry. No wonder he wanted to leave the fundraiser in such a hurry. Darn it, Brianne had to show up—but it wasn't uncommon for her to create havoc.

Worse, Kate had been on the job one day, and she'd already let Rosa down. Her friend would be so disappointed if this whole venture failed before it started, because her business was on the line this time.

He cursed under his breath. "You have some fast explaining to do. Spill it!"

Kate held her hands up in surrender. "Okay, yes, I am Rosa's friend. Is it so far-fetched that I can also be a client and the match she made for you?" Her voice came out squeaky and high-pitched. She was a terrible liar.

"You are playing me, woman! And you'd better admit it before I lose my temper and phone my lawyers."

She'd known from the beginning this was a bad idea. How should she handle the fallout without Cole resorting to legal proceedings? "Okay, I'm sorry, but we have an excellent reason for what we've done. I'm sure once you hear the entire story, you'll understand."

"I'm just tired of all the games. Maybe I'm just plain tired." He ran a hand over his eyes and sighed.

His admission surprised her.

"I haven't taken a vacation in five years, and I think tonight I hit the wall." He ran a hand through his thick brown hair. "And I find out I'm being scammed by someone whose credentials are supposed to be impeccable. What is it? Billions of dollars too much to resist?"

Oooh, the man was such an idiot. She wanted to slap him, but considering how angry he was right now, maybe not the best idea. "I promise you we have an explainable reason for—"

"There'd better be," he cut in.

She could see in his eyes he imagined she wanted the same thing everyone else did. Money-money-money. "Cole Prentice, you'd better listen because I'll be honest." She bit her lip. Dear heaven, let this be the right thing to do.

He shifted his position in the limo, then tapped the privacy button. The glass shut between them and the driver. "That would be very refreshing."

His tone had become droll and caustic. "I am Rosa's best friend. I'm doing this as a favor. Not to become your soul mate, but to determine whether you're serious about wanting someone—an actual soul mate."

She considered his statement. He'd exuded confidence, and yet, his fingers tapped on the leather seat. *A nervous gesture?* "I would think the hefty down payment would be evidence enough."

His intent, dark eyes glittered. "So, you aren't interested in me?"

"Sorry, but no. I'm here to provide a service." She planted her arms over her chest.

His eyebrows tented. He looked her up and down.

"Not that kind of service!"

"What kind then?"

His tone sliced through her. He was angry, and she couldn't blame him. He'd just admitted he'd hit the wall. Now she was telling him everything about her being here was a sham. Not the end of the world, because he'd already figured that out.

With little hope of telling him in a way that wouldn't upset him, she inhaled. "Rosa is a very astute judge of people. She figured you didn't want a mate.

She thought you were searching for someone temporary to soften your image." Kate shrugged and gave him a regretful smile. "Rosa was afraid if she lined you up with an actual client, you'd both be in for a major disappointment. That wouldn't be good for your personal relations, especially if the client-in-question talked about it afterwards. Don't forget, any woman chosen as a match for you also pays the hefty matchmaking fee. She'll expect results. With that in mind, Rosa devised a plan to find out what you need before she could find the perfect person." She had his undivided attention now, and he wasn't giving away any emotion. She didn't know what kind of mess she was getting herself into.

"And you? Why did you agree to this?"

"I told you, Rosa and I are friends." His dead calm voice sent shivers through her.

He nodded, but his eyes narrowed. "You owe her, don't you?"

Kate swallowed. "I do. But I would have helped her, anyway. We're friends."

Cole leaned forward for the intercom. "Frank, take us to my office."

"What? Why?" Kate pressed her hands into the car seat.

"We have some serious business to discuss, Ms. Cameron."

Kate's heart plunged to a stutter. Could things get any worse?

Chapter Four

With limited time before they got to the office, Kate had to at least do damage control before Cole contacted Rosa and fired them. As much as she'd rather go home and consult with Rosa, she needed to make this work tonight. She followed him into his office.

Once inside, Cole stripped off his jacket and threw it on a red leather couch against one wall. He paced to this desk and flicked on the green desk lamp, then plunked into the massive antique leather executive chair.

She stood frozen in the doorway.

He motioned for her to sit in the chair opposite his desk.

Like a truant student at the principal's office in high school, she complied. "Rosa is a professional, Mr. Prentice." *Kate needed a way out of this.* "She wouldn't go against the contract you signed. And, I'm sure you noted, there were no guarantees every match will work out. Besides, just because Rosa and I are friends doesn't mean you and I wouldn't make a good match." Her spirits sank. Had she just said that?

One of his eyebrows arched. "You're saying you want to make this work between us?"

She glanced to the floor in an instant. Good grief, she was a worse liar than an actress. "Sorry, but no. To be honest, I'm not a huge fan of people with money."

Surprised she'd been so frank, she'd probably made things much worse.

His eyes narrowed. "Why do you dislike people with money?"

With a sharp inhalation, she sat ramrod in her chair. "I have my reasons. None of which are any of your business. If you prefer someone else, that can be easily remedied. If you don't want another client, I will carry out Rosa's contract for two weeks. I will be the best date I can be when we're in the public eye."

"And when we're not?"

His voice reverberated through her. "Now that you know how I feel, I won't have to pretend. I believe honesty is the best policy."

He choked back a laugh. "If that's true, why wasn't I told you were Rosa's best friend? You might as well quit bamboozling me. You're not very proficient."

Bamboozle? *Who uses words like that?* "I don't understand. Do you believe whether I want a relationship with you is relevant? Are you saying you want a relationship?" She frowned. She sprang to her feet and leaned forward, with hands planted on his desk. "Besides, if I'm not the person to help fix your media profile, I'm sure Rosa will be more than happy to find another match." She echoed his haughty gaze but failed when his deep brown eyes drilled into her.

At least when his mouth quirked, his features softened, a little. "Shall I call her and ask for a new match, Mr. Prentice? Did Rosa misread the situation? Are you hoping for love?" *Had she ground a little too much salt into his wounds*?

He covered his mouth with one hand, to hide a laugh.

The nerve! Kate gritted her teeth against saying something she shouldn't and stepped back from his desk. She should tell him where to go, then march out the door. On a normal day, she would have done just that—if Rosa wasn't the reason she was here.

It surprised her when he smiled without hiding it, a genuine smile, and not sarcastic.

Weird, at this intense moment, she considered him to be handsome in a rough-edged, sophisticated way. She had to get a grip. She stared at the ceiling and counted to ten. She had to do something to maintain composure.

Leaning forward with elbows on his desk, he continued staring with two fingers against his bottom lip.

"Listen! I don't care how much money you have or how much power you wield. Why did you force me to come to your office?" She glanced down at the beautiful gown. The gown he'd bought without blinking at the cost. Tiny crystal sequins reflected and refracted the soft night-time lighting of Cole's office, reminding her of twinkling stars. No way would she squirm. That was what he wanted. At least, he hadn't picked up the phone to call Rosa—but then, he hadn't told her what he planned to do, yet.

He continued to stare without speaking.

Uncomfortable under his scrutiny, she strode to the window and stared out at the cityscape. Distancing herself from Cole Prentice gave her time to come to terms with everything that happened. How had one innocent encounter with an old university acquaintance caused everything to go so wrong?

She ran one hand over her hip in a nervous gesture

and glanced toward him over her shoulder. His current silent treatment was unnerving—and he used it to his advantage. "I'm not staying here much longer, so you might as well tell me what you intend to do." She straightened her back.

Cole spun his chair around, accessed a cupboard behind his desk, and retrieved two square-cut crystal glasses and a bottle of scotch. He set the glasses on his desk and poured. "I think we should have a drink first."

Her throat tightened. She summoned all the composure she could muster to watch while he poured. His expensive, black watch drew her gaze to his hands. Better to gaze at his hands, than to be confused by that smile again. She hated that he exuded power and self-confidence.

He offered a glass.

She took it.

Angry electricity arced between them.

She wrapped both hands around the crystal as if her life depended on it.

Muscles bunched in his jaw.

Negating his feigned indifference, and proving less than impervious to the situation as he wanted to project, she'd gained back a little of her own power, and she narrowed her gaze.

He swirled the amber liquid in his glass, taking a moment to smell the aroma before he took a sip. "I'm curious."

She'd have sensed his penetrating gaze even in the pitch dark.

"What are you planning to do? Lead me on? Make me fall for you?"

His words were soft, but uncompromising. A

person didn't have to read the headlines to know this master-of-his-own-domain wasn't a man to mess with. She bit her lip. "Of course not. As soon as she discovered your seriousness about a relationship, Rosa would set you up with a legitimate client."

He frowned.

Shoot, terrible choice of words—*quotations in the air*—legitimate. Her stomach tightened.

"How many times have you done this before?"

"Never."

He appeared unconvinced, until his expression changed to something she couldn't read. And that scared her even more.

"What if I decided I wanted you?" He stepped closer. "Are you even single? Available?"

While he waited for her answer, his mouth set in a firm line. But, his unadulterated attention to her body caused some weird, have-me-if-you-want-me feelings that should never happen. Either way, she didn't want to come up against someone like him because she'd lose—in more ways than one.

He lifted his glass and took a longer drink.

That gave Kate a chance to come back to earth. "You are the most insulting, insufferable man I've ever met. Of course I'm single, but I'm not interested in you. Not in the least. I'm sure you already know that. I haven't tried to hide that fact." She squeezed her hands into fists. She hated he could irritate her with such ease. "The contract stipulates both parties must agree regarding a relationship, so I'm not telling you anything you don't know. And, for your information, my feelings don't breach the contract."

Her shoulders bunched when he ignored her last

statement.

Leaning against the corner of his desk, he picked up a remote control and pointed it at the wall behind her.

When a fireplace flicked on, Kate froze. If he fancied he could blackmail her into a seduction scene, he would be very sorry. She forced herself not to show anger. "And yes, I'm single. Not that it's any of your concern."

"And…" He mimicked her tone. "I reiterate, what if I decided I wanted you?"

With her chest tightening, she let out a slow exhalation, while squeezing her hands into tight balls. "You'd be out of luck. I will never agree to being your match." His dark brown eyes stared into hers, this time, without malice. She had a feeling the truth of the situation had been a red flag.

He tipped his head to one side. "Help me out here, Kate. Rosa realized what kind of trouble this could cause if I found out about the deception?"

Heat built behind Kate's eyes. Damn it, don't cry now! "She didn't mean you any harm. She was being the best matchmaker for you. Her instincts make her the best, and she's seldom wrong. I'm sorry if that's not the case with you."

He strode to the fireplace.

Even though her instincts shot into full flight mode, she maintained outward composure.

"To be honest, she is correct." He leaned closer.

His words slid out in a way she almost missed their meaning. Given his earlier reaction to her confession, his body language made little sense. "I beg your pardon?"

"You are right. I have no interest in a full-time love match. That's not to say we can't have a little fun, on the side."

Anger burned in her stomach, but she bit back the acrid words forming. Even more frustrating, he pressed closer, his body heat mingled with her own, creating tiny electrical flares across her arms. She exhaled. She hadn't even realized she'd been holding her breath.

He'd just admitted that Rosa had been correct about his intentions. How could he possibly hold anything against her after that? *Thank you, thank you.* She calmed herself before speaking. "That's good news then."

He shook his head. "Don't think just because Rosa was correct about me, she had the right to send you, instead of a client. The contract is specific. It stipulates that you are a vetted client of her company, which I assume you are not?"

Kate froze. Her silent jubilation had been short-lived. She didn't answer him. So far, their little white lie hadn't worked very well.

"As I suspected."

Anger ignited anew behind his intimidating eyes.

After a sharp inhale, he stared at his glass. "Neither of you are out of the woods, yet."

That doused her millisecond of relief. "Why can't you understand that Rosa wanted to make sure you got what you wanted? She takes her job with extreme seriousness."

"I take fraud the same way."

Fraud? *Deep trouble.* She scrambled for her phone, then realized she'd left it at home. It didn't fit in her tiny sequined purse. "Why don't I call Rosa? She can explain the situation better than I can." She extended a hand for his phone.

"Don't!"

The sharpness of his voice made her spine lock. "Why not?"

"I don't need Rosa to discuss how this will happen."

His quiet voice held little emotion—that scared Kate more than any threat. "What will happen?"

"You and me."

"Oh, no! No. No. No." His serious expression, along with his air of determination, shocked her. It obliterated any chance of getting herself out of this mess—or escape.

"Yes. Yes. Yes."

Kate squirmed. His firm tone brooked no denial.

"Either that, or you and your matchmaker friend will be involved in a very public, very nasty fraud charge. I'm sure you don't want to do that to your friend—or yourself."

Her heart thumped inside her chest—being sued would ruin Rosa's business and her own. "That's so unfair."

He laughed, but no humor reached his eyes.

"Unfair to whom? You have obligated yourself, and now you are here worming your way, in public, as my date. You will fulfill your contract, or I'll sue both of you. I imagine you've already realized that being sued for fraud can ruin your cupcake enterprise—In fact, I can make very sure of it."

Blood coagulated in her veins, and her head swam. He had done his homework. And he was the frozen food king who'd be willing to ruin her.

The lines near his mouth deepened. "I see this bit of information has made the situation more real."

"You son-of-a…"

"So, it would seem." He let out a slow breath.

"You said you'd read media articles about me. Well, here I am, Ms. Cameron. In the flesh. You will not take advantage of me. In fact, you've made a very grave error in judgment if you think a pretty face and curvy body can sweet-talk me into being duped."

She opened her mouth to correct him, but nothing came out. Curvy body? No one had ever said that before. And, how could that be the take away from his threat? She needed help.

"Your obvious attributes, however, will sweeten the pot. The media likes nothing more than seeing a beautiful woman on my arm. You *will* continue with this charade, for as long as I tell you, or default in our written agreement."

She raised a hand to slap his face, but he caught her wrist and yanked her toward him until she pressed against his chest.

One arm wrapped around her, and his hand rested on the small of her back. "That wouldn't be very nice, my dear. Violence doesn't suit you. Besides, you'd better get used to me telling you what to do, because you and I will be very close over the next two weeks."

"Not unless hell freezes over!" she gritted out.

"Funny you'd mention freezing." His gaze burned into hers, his lips so close.

Why did she notice his dark hair had been trimmed since their last encounter, and his whiter-than-white shirt unbuttoned to show the sprinkling of hair near his neckline? She couldn't deny his masculinity, even though she detested him.

"Don't forget, according to the papers, if anyone can freeze hell over, I can." His mouth formed a thin line.

He couldn't be serious. For the moment, she was cornered. At least until she could figure this thing out. She needed to consult Rosa. Maybe a lawyer. For now, she'd go along, as long as he kept his hands to himself.

She shoved away and strengthened her resolve. She could do this, had to do this, for Rosa, and for her own business. Kate's stomach tightened. She hadn't been wrong about rich men. They were always power brokers and takers.

"That's what I expected you to say."

His words made her grit her teeth.

"I think it's even better now that we're being up front with each other. Now, you know the ground rules." His fake smile faded, and he ran two fingers along the edge of her chin.

She twisted her face away. "I'll pretend to be your girlfriend for the time being, but if you think you can blackmail me into doing anything that compromises my morals, you'd better think again."

While enduring his heart-stopping focus, reminding her of his powerful ambitions, she steeled her spine, then pressed her lips together and inhaled. Perhaps, she could've handled the situation better.

"Do we understand each other?"

His tone sent shivers through to her core. She looked away.

"Besides, even though everything about the two of us being together is fake, I'm sure you've noticed we have some wicked chemistry. So, it shouldn't be a total waste of our time."

She couldn't believe he'd just hinted that they could take advantage of their situation with no strings attached. "Dream on!" Worse, the way he wielded his wealth and power over her reminded her of her ex-fiancé. She could very well imagine Rodney blackmailing women into giving him sexual favors. Her stomach flipped, and she swallowed against sudden nausea.

Kate glanced around. Her attention settled on a door next to the fireplace. If he had a bachelor's make-out room behind that door, she was out of here, no matter what the consequences. "What's behind that door?"

He blinked.

If nothing else, her question seemed to surprise him.

"Lavatory." He frowned. "Help yourself."

"Are you sure?" Her voice let him know she didn't believe him. She stalked to the door and yanked it open. It was a small room with a toilet and sink.

"As I said, it is a lavatory."

While embarrassed that she'd expected he had a make-out room in his office similar to the one her ex-fiancé had, she had no intention of explaining why she'd been relieved to see his executive-style lavatory. The small room matched the décor in the rest of his office right down to the soft inset lighting in the copper tray ceiling. Cole's office had an impressive red Italian leather sofa, padded executive and desk chairs, and original watercolor paintings—most were bright urban art that highlighted his taste. His desk was polished and clear of the usual items other than one gold pen and one tray of paperwork. He liked his things tidy.

He slid up behind her. "Tell me, what did you expect to find behind that door?"

His breath brushed her ear. "Nothing. It doesn't matter."

"Oh, I think it matters. We'll spend more time together over the next while; we need to be honest. Or, as honest as you can manage."

Her gut twisted, and anger spiked her blood pressure. "I'm always honest!"

One of his eyebrows lifted, and her face burned against her will. Darn him.

He strode to his desk and opened a folder. "By the way, we're going on vacation."

"What? No. I can't. I have a business," she began.

"Except you're on vacation for the next two weeks." He tapped one finger on her profile sheet. "Don't forget I've paid a pretty penny for the privilege."

She leaned over to see the contents of his folder.

But he slapped it closed.

She very much doubted Rosa would mention anything about Rodney. Either way, her previous failed relationship wasn't a secret. Anyone could do an Internet search and read all about it—even though the reports had been one hundred percent lies.

Just having the chance to find out what he wanted from a matchmaker wouldn't have been a big deal. Then she would have reported back to Rosa. Now she was stuck for two weeks. Her stomach twisted again.

Kate decided he hadn't done the search on her ex-fiancé yet. *Good grief.* Why had she agreed to be his date? She should have realized her history with Rodney could put Rosa's business at risk, too.

"And, you *will* help salvage my image," he added.

"You could always get a dog."

"See, that's what I like about you. You have a wicked, albeit misplaced, sense of humor. You aren't afraid to stand up to me, even under circumstances like this."

"I don't intend to make this blackmail pleasant, Mr. Prentice. So, don't get any ideas. I'll play the part in public, but in private, you'll find out just how much I loathe you."

He laughed. "I find you a breath of fresh air, Ms. Cameron."

"Having a girlfriend won't make people forget about your bad image."

"Touché. But I think you're wrong. It'll amaze you how fast the papers will go from assassinating my character to speculating on my love life. *Our love life.* Imagine how the media will play out our relationship." He grinned.

Her condemnation did little to ding him. "I'm afraid I don't follow?"

"I'm the meat and potatoes man—albeit frozen. You're the dessert."

The way he surveyed her made her feel like dessert right now, too, thanks to the gorgeous dress. And, as the main dish, his handsome outward appearance worked to his benefit. Too bad, the media had him pegged—a first-class jerk. "I have to go." She wished she hadn't attempted a good deed for her friend. Oh, she should be on vacation all right, but alone—not with someone who believed he had bought her body and her silence with his payment to Rosa.

"Get packed. We leave on Monday." He slammed the folder on the desk.

"What? Wait. That's two days away!" He tipped his head in a thoughtful pose that she didn't believe.

"I was thinking about San Francisco."

"You're kidding!" *I'll have no backup in another city. I'll be too far from Rosa to call for help. Not that I'm not strong enough to look after myself.* She closed her eyes and braced for whatever happened next.

Chapter Five

After their meeting in his office, Cole drove Kate home. She'd said she'd have preferred to call a taxi, but he'd insisted he drive. He appreciated her silence in her corner of the sports car. He needed time to devise a plan.

Lady luck had delivered her. Having someone attempt to scam him suited his purposes. He had every intention of putting on a good show for the world, but he didn't want to complicate his life with a woman who'd expect more than he wanted to give. Now, he could have the best of both worlds. A significant other with no strings. His board would accept the news, and the media might leave him alone, for a while.

One minor glitch—the way he'd physically reacted to the stolen kiss at the fundraiser. He was thankful Kate didn't like him. He gritted his teeth. She and Rosa had tried to play him.

He walked her to the door and waited for her to enter her apartment. The paparazzi could be anywhere. She'd be alone and vulnerable, and they could mob her. He bit his lip and grimaced. If things were different, and he hadn't found out about her deception, *would she have invited him in*?

"Good night."

"Night."

She had an expected edge of irritation in her voice.

Nonplussed, he waited for her to unlock the door. When a camera lens reflected off a streetlight, Cole's practiced gaze spotted the paparazzo right away. With one quick move, he blocked her from the lens. "Kate, don't look behind me, okay?"

With key still in her hand, she tilted her head up and frowned. "Why not? Don't tell me the paparazzi know where I live, too?"

He nodded. "It's unfortunate, but by now, they know everything about you." In his experience, most people would have peered around him right away.

"Great. This just gets better and better." She frowned and stared at her key.

"Given that we are being watched, we can't just shake hands and say goodnight without making waves."

Her eyes narrowed.

He expected her protest, so he leaned down and kissed her just to get it over with. At first, a light touch to make the paparazzo believe they were on an actual date, but the kiss exploded into something hotter than hell.

Even though he'd meant to put on a show for the media, he felt the ground becoming less solid as their kiss deepened. His arms circled her. She didn't hide the fact she detested him, but their palpable chemistry drove him to distraction all evening.

When she shoved a hand against his chest to make him back off, she gasped for air.

Heck, so did he.

"I think he got the pictures he wanted." She ran an index finger across her bottom lip.

Considering Cole had blackmailed her, she'd hate allowing him to kiss her. She'd surprised him. "Get some sleep. You've got a busy day ahead of you tomorrow."

"Busy? You said we were leaving in two days." Her mouth thinned, and her eyes narrowed.

"I don't want to leave you alone for two days to think of a way out of this." He forced a light laugh. "You and I will be very close for the next while. Can you be ready at ten a.m.?"

"Not sure that'll work."

"Not sure you have a choice." He allowed a hint of dry amusement in his voice.

"I could go to the paparazzi right now and tell them what a reprobate you are."

Cole laughed out loud this time. "You wouldn't be telling them anything they don't already know." He lowered his voice and hated himself for what he'd say next. "You'd be furthering the demise of your own business, though."

"Jerk." She turned to unlock her door. "I'm pretty sure you'll be sorry you cornered me into this." She stepped inside and slammed the door in his face.

Let the paparazzi get pictures of that! On the way home, he considered his next week with Kate Cameron. If only he could delete Kate's expression of abject terror when he'd threatened her business. What was wrong with him? Had he turned into his father overnight?

His stomach clenched, as he pulled into his garage. She was right. He was a jerk. He'd resorted to blackmail, something he'd never done before, and he couldn't believe he was doing it. Kate turned out to be the perfect woman for this charade. Things couldn't have worked out better if he'd rigged it himself. He didn't care if she was interested in him. Their encounters were a business deal, period.

An image of her in the gown seared the edges of his consciousness against his will. He'd all but burst into flames when he'd leaned down to enter the limo and spotted her in that gown. He couldn't imagine how a woman with her beauty, her bod, and her brains didn't have a man already locked in.

Good thing she couldn't read his mind—he'd be in big trouble. Besides, she was better off without a cold-hearted guy like him, who'd resort to blackmail to keep her in line. He picked up the phone and dialed. His executive assistant answered after the fourth ring. "Evans, I want to fly to San Francisco tomorrow."

"Cole? Is that you?"

The man sounded groggy, and Cole gritted his teeth. He'd phoned too late, and the man had been asleep. Cole seldom did this to his employee, but darn it, this was an emergency. "Who else would ask you to book my private jet?" He held up an arm to check the time.

"Sure thing, boss. Just a second. I'll get my glasses on and take down the details before I call the airport."

"Take the next week off, Evans. I'll be away." Cole liked to thank his employees for off-hours work. Being a billionaire business executive sometimes required ignoring etiquette, but he at least tried to make it up to his employees with little perks here and there.

"Not a problem, Mr. Prentice. Have a good night."

Cole could hear the grin in Evan's voice. Evans, no doubt, expected Kate was spending the night. He wanted to laugh. She was the one woman on the planet who wouldn't cave because he had money. At least, he hoped that was true.

Chapter Six

That night, sitting on the side of her bed, Kate told Rosa about her nightmare date with Cole and how he'd found out about them. "What will we do about this fiasco?"

Rosa remained silent at the other end for a few beats. "I've gotten us into a mess this time, haven't I?"

Kate's chest tightened. "We can figure this thing out, Rosa. That arrogant billionaire will not take down the two of us. Not without a fight."

"But he's got so much money behind him, Kate. I'm not sure we can win against him, if he wants to cause trouble."

Rosa never accepted defeat—ever. This was worse than Kate realized. If Cole Prentice wanted to ruin them, he could do so in a heartbeat. She imagined the headlines... *Matchmaker uses fraudulent tactics to reel in billionaire.*

Kate wished they had the situation under control. She had no choice but to stick to her promise, as distasteful as it might be. She'd have to maintain self-control against the arrogant billionaire, whose primary goal was to use her and to make her pay for her well-meaning deception.

Guilt wracked her about deceiving him—until he forced her to go along with the charade. He hadn't done anything to change her opinion of him. Probably just as well. She didn't plan to make their time together easy or friendly.

The next day, after a few hours of less-than-restful sleep, Kate seated herself and locked her seatbelt on Cole's private jet with its plush interiors, soft leather recliners, a wide screen television, and bar. *I'm not impressed.* She rolled her eyes.

Did Cole appreciate what he had? He'd been born rich and hadn't experienced poverty. She'd bet he did not know what having his business threatened meant, either.

"Would you like a drink?" a slim attendant asked.

"Two coffees and some of those buttery Danishes you whip up." Cole smiled at the young woman.

"Of course, sir." The young blonde's cheeks suffused with color.

"May I bend to your will while I'm at it, sir?" Kate stared out her cabin window. Cole had pinned her on the inside. Several empty seats remained in the spacious cabin, but he remained too close.

"I'm not deaf. And, yes, you may."

"Fat chance."

He chuckled.

She bit the inside of her lip. No way would she give him the satisfaction of thinking she found him amusing, because she did not. "I still don't understand why we need to go to San Francisco? The press is just as available in Boston."

"If we're lucky, there'll be no press to follow us around in San Francisco."

Her wide-eyed expression met his. "Isn't the purpose of this charade to fool the press into thinking you have a heart and a soul?"

He winced. "I have my reasons. But, never fear, the paparazzi will find us sooner than later, so don't get too comfortable." He nudged her elbow. "You'll have to put on a splendid show."

"Goody." She yanked her arm away and planted her hands on her lap. *He did not know the hell she would rain down!*

His expression narrowed. "You'll play nice, won't you? You can carry this thing off." He held up one hand, then motioned toward the flight attendant heading in their direction with steaming coffee in china cups and saucers. "If you can't convince my staff, then…"

"If I'm not an excellent actor, then you'll have to let me go."

Cole laughed. "No. Then *you'll* pay the price."

Flames of frustration clotted inside Kate's chest, constricting her breathing. She'd never screamed in public, never threw a hissy fit, but she wanted to right now. She hated to be out of control of her own life again. Until Rosa found a way out, she'd have to play along, but she didn't have to be accommodating.

"Thank you, Ginny. This is lovely." Cole smiled at the attendant and took the tray.

Kate suppressed the urge to roll her eyes.

Ginny waited. "Is there anything else I can do, sir?"

"No, we're fine. I've got it from here." Cole placed the tray on a table, then handed a steaming mug to Kate.

Kate smiled at the young woman to prove to Cole that she could carry off the façade if she wanted. She took a sip. "It's very good, thank you."

"You're welcome."

Her voice sounded like a little girl. *Nails-on-a-chalkboard* to Kate. "Let me guess, new employee?" Kate watched the woman sway down the aisle. She'd probably throw a hip out by putting any more effort into her exit. A fact Cole hadn't missed. He had a stupid grin on his face that Kate wanted to smack right off.

"How'd you guess?"

"I'd guess that's one you haven't slept with—yet."

He kept smiling, but the twinkle in his eyes turned to ice. "You have a very low opinion of me, Ms. Cameron. Even the media hasn't tarnished me with quite so damning a brush."

His voice scraped over her like steel wool.

"I don't make a habit of sleeping with my employees. Not that it's any business of yours."

"You're right. I should apologize. But I won't. Just because you're a blackmailer, why would I think such mean things?"

"You act as if you've done nothing wrong." Cole snatched her hand in his and maintained his gentle, but firm, grasp.

He'd never manhandled her yet, but he made it obvious things should go his way. He opened her fist, one finger at a time, and lifted her palm to his mouth. The moment his lips touched, she yanked back. He maintained his hold without being forceful.

"Uh uh, this is part of your test. You wouldn't want my staff to think you don't like me."

"They're probably used to women who are only with you for your money." She regretted her words right away. She wasn't deliberately mean, ever. Worse, she'd been called a fortune hunter by the media, and she'd hated it.

He let her extract her hand, and she stared out the window. Regretful tears burned behind her lids, while her hand still tingled from his touch. Reacting to his touch didn't make sense. She didn't like him, so why had her body betrayed her? Pretending to like him would be a lot harder than she'd hoped. *She wanted to run away*.

She had to remember, from his perspective, she and Rosa had tried to trick him. If he sued Rosa for breach of contract, the damage could mean disaster. And it would be so unfair. Rosa always did the very best for her clients. Kate mulled over her situation.

The captain's voice addressed them over the intercom system. "Mr. Prentice and guest, please buckle your seatbelts. We'll be landing soon."

For once, she didn't care he could use his wealth and power to hustle them through the airport. They were in the limo within a few minutes. She'd have leaned forward in her seat to glimpse the Golden Gate Bridge in the distance, but she didn't want to give him the satisfaction of knowing she'd never been here before.

Glad he'd been quiet since they'd climbed into the limo, she didn't want to be the one who broke the peaceful silence. Besides, he seemed preoccupied with his cell phone. His hands were messaging at breakneck speed, with his head tipped and his brow furrowed.

As they arrived at the hotel, and the limo eased to a stop, Cole tucked his phone away.

The hotel staff approached them in a flurry of excitement before the driver got out and opened her door.

She had to remember Cole was a billionaire staying

at their hotel—what couldn't his money buy?

Her, for one.

Since he'd kissed her hand on the plane, she'd been in emotional turmoil. She couldn't stand this rich, egocentric billionaire who was blackmailing her, so why had the kiss affected her? He could attempt to seduce her, but no matter his tactic, it wouldn't work. She'd already suffered false accusations from her ex-fiancé, Rodney. Going through anything like that again would be intolerable—this whole thing could blow up in her face.

While they followed the bellman, Cole rested his left hand against the small of her back in a proprietary manner.

Her muscles strained against his touch. She was trapped, unless she could convince him she'd been helping Rosa who had the best intentions. What kind of man would take advantage of a situation like that? She bit her lip. She'd read what type of man he was. The papers were full of his cold, calculating business acumen. Nothing about his warm, forgiving persona had been printed.

Cole's expression remained impenetrable. He hadn't glanced her way since they left the limo. At least that gave her a little clarity to think straight. To plan her own way out of this mess. When there'd been no mention of a second room, she wanted to run as they headed to the elevator bank. He wouldn't go *that* far.

Seeing the bellman open their door, she stepped inside and surveyed the room. She saw one king-sized bed and a seating area. Panic surged. Not about to happen! She opened her mouth to let Cole have it in stereo.

The hotel employee opened an adjoining door between their rooms. "Your room, madam."

She noted he wiped off the quick grin when her expression changed to a glare. Worse, she noted the humor in Cole's eyes at her reaction. Acid burned in her stomach. She attempted to escape and shut the door.

He leaned against the doorframe, a half-smile on his lips. "I'm not quite as bad as you seem to think."

She blew out a calming breath, disparaging herself. How could she, even for a minute, think he could be kind?

"Can you be ready for dinner, in say..." He lifted his right arm and peered at his expensive watch. "Half an hour? I made reservations yesterday."

"I can." *He'd probably hate her bargain store wardrobe.* She didn't own any clothes that cost thousands of dollars. And, she'd sent his designer gown back to his office by courier yesterday. "How should I dress?"

"Let's be casual tonight. We'll go to John's Place. A nice little restaurant where Dashiel Hammett used to go in his heyday. The seafood is excellent there."

The last thing Kate wanted to do right now was eat anything. Her stomach swirled with worry. Speaking of Dashiel Hammett, she would like to clobber Cole with the Maltese Falcon. Meanwhile, he acted as if she were his actual girlfriend. No doubt, he found it easier to play it that way and less stressful—except she despised him and his blackmailing ways. Until she had a nefarious plan of her own. *Could she go through with it?*

She stepped closer, frizzling inside with nervousness. Could she carry this off? She touched his bare forearm with one hand. If she went overboard, then he'd be suspicious.

He jumped back. "What's wrong with you? We're alone. You don't have to pretend."

"Why not? I'm not immune to your obvious charm when you deign to share it." *She gagged inside.* "I think you might have a soul underneath all your armor."

He laughed.

She wanted to slap him—hard.

His mouth thinned. "I don't know what your game is now, Kate, but I prefer it when in private, your distaste for me shines through. Please don't insult me by making me think you want to spend even one second with me. I know better."

Now she understood the feeling was mutual. She slumped her shoulders in relief. "You're wrong, of course."

"Am I?" His voice changed, softened, and he leaned closer.

"Yes," she squeaked, doing her own backing away right now.

He grasped her by the shoulders. "So, what would happen if I did this…"

Too late. His head lowered, and he captured her lips with perfect timing—just when she began to open her mouth to speak. He deepened the kiss with such expertise the room began to spin. A hint of spiced cologne entered her consciousness, while his hands settled on her waist.

Pressing her hands against his hard, soldier-of-business-fortune body made every nerve ending tingle. She had to struggle to catch her breath. Panic made her gather whatever strength she had left. She braced her hands on his biceps and shoved.

He held tight.

Her inability to force distance between them did even more damage to her shattered nerves, her body betraying her at every touch of his body. Unable to think, she drifted her hands up to his shoulders and wrapped her arms around his neck. *She'd show him!* Wasn't this her addle-minded plan, anyway?

Except, when his lips touched hers again, realization broke through her moment of madness. If she could seduce him, to get out of her predicament... *No, she was deluding herself.* He'd already seen through her initial naïve plan. She stepped away, gritting her teeth against his self-satisfied expression.

Lesson learned—never try to outmaneuver him again.

His kisses were deadly weapons, and she had no ammunition against him. Remembering his very serious threats against her and Rosa shouldn't have been difficult.

"I'm not sure why you wanted to do this, but just so you know, I am not averse to practicing, in order to convince the paparazzi."

He sounded angry, though, and stepped back. Her blood boiled, but he'd shaken her. She adjusted her shoulder-length hair and cleared her throat. "Now that we've got that out of the way, we don't have to pretend any longer."

"Riiiight." He stretched the word out.

"I need to get ready for dinner." She crossed her arms over her chest. "And, from now on in private, keep your hands off of me."

"Okay, but only if you don't try to seduce me again." He tipped his head and winked. "I like it better when you tell the truth."

What was wrong with her? *Crazy, crazy woman.* Futility burned hot in her gut, welling up to the point her hands shook. If she were honest, she deserved the last crack after saying she had to pretend to like him. She'd hurt his ego, and he'd lashed back. She edged past him.

But he'd blocked the door and wouldn't budge.

"Jerk." She planted her hands on her hips. "I'm tired of your games. If you keep this up, I'm going home. To hell with your threats."

"Now, that's more like it." He laughed. "This is how I expect you to treat me when we're alone. At least I know this is honest."

"You're impossible." She twisted her hands together.

He slid aside. "Be ready to put on a very good show tonight. After all, it's what you're being paid for. And I don't want to be late."

He'd spoken through gritted teeth, but in the end, he sounded tired. Exhausted, more like it. Who'd have guessed that someday she'd be bought and paid for— trapped. The second he'd moved, she slammed the door between them, grabbed a pillow off the oversized bed, and tossed it at the door. The hit created a soft puff— something like her attempt to trick him—ineffective and not very satisfying. Even though she wanted to, she couldn't break anything in this expensive room.

He'd taught her a valuable lesson. She was too inexperienced to play games with the expert billionaire. Staring at the phone on the bedstand, she considered calling Rosa to quit. She gritted her teeth and reconsidered. He wouldn't make her run home crying.

Her upbringing had forced her to be stronger than that.

Besides, she had a secret weapon to maintain sanity. All she had to do to dredge up a cold dash of reality by thinking of her millionaire ex-fiancé, Rodney Hollander III.

Their wedding had been two weeks away when he'd suggested she sign for the venue because he was in a meeting. The venue manager had emphasized there'd be no refunds, before she'd signed the document. *Had he known more about Rodney than her?* Everyone seemed to have been aware of Rodney's philandering, except her.

Rodney had sent a *Dear Jane* email the next day. When she'd told him about the bill, he'd ignored her. And, since her signature had been on the non-refundable bill, she'd been left holding a fifty-thousand-dollar invoice. She'd have lost her business without Rosa's loan.

Before becoming Rodney's fiancé, she'd garnered coverage of her cupcake company in several magazines. She'd been on a short-list for the entrepreneur of the year until the media got wind of their nasty breakup.

She'd been the one vilified, even though Rodney had been cheating while they were engaged. Learning he told the media the breakup was her fault broke her heart. He'd implied she was nothing but a gold digger, and her cupcake sales had taken a massive dive. Two years passed before her business came back from the bad press.

Her business was on an upward trend again. She sighed. In order to help Rosa, she'd put herself in the crosshairs of the same type of bad press again. If Cole dragged her through the mire, her business would never survive.

Twenty-five minutes later, when Cole knocked on their adjoining door, she was ready—and she'd steadied her resolve. Her goal for the evening meant she must stay calm and give him no opportunities to throw her off guard. If everything progressed well, she'd hear from Rosa tomorrow, and she could tell Cole Prentice to take a royal leap off the Golden Gate Bridge into the shark-infested waters below. She opened the door and stepped into the thick carpeted hallway, with rich burgundy tones on the walls and prints of famous San Francisco artists, as indicated on the brass plaques underneath.

He eyed her up and down and raised a rakish eyebrow.

The move looked as if nothing had happened moments ago.

"You are beautiful tonight."

"I'm afraid my wardrobe is pretty simple." She brushed one hand over her knee-length flowery summer dress.

"It's lovely."

She didn't like to stare, but he portrayed the perfect billionaire dressed in casual, but expensive jeans, and a white polo shirt that enhanced his tan.

"Shall we go?" He held the door, then led the way to the elevator.

They didn't speak on the way down.

In the lobby, a young man said "hello" while his gaze roamed over her in a predatory way.

Cole glared at the man.

The grin wiped off the man's face, and he left without a word.

"You didn't have to be rude." She bit her lip.

"I didn't say a word."

"Your glare was enough to make most people run in fear."

He grinned. "Think so? As far as the world knows, Ms. Cameron." He leaned forward for her alone. "You are mine. A naïve idiot like him is lucky I didn't escort him outside and teach him a lesson for his brazen actions."

"That's just Neanderthal thinking." Kate wanted to expand on her dislike of his comment, but what was the point? He'd say whatever he liked and didn't care what she thought.

"Men who give a damn don't allow other males to insult their date by leering."

To be honest, Cole's reaction hadn't been aggressive. The way the young man had stared had made her uncomfortable. Strange, Cole Prentice had just defended her, even though he believed she was a gold-digger. Rodney could've cared less when other men ogled her. In fact, he liked it.

"Let's get going. We don't want to miss our reservation." Cole moved toward the lobby door.

Outside, a white limo about a block long was waiting at the curb.

Somehow, she didn't see him using this mode of transportation when he was alone. Maybe that's what his dates expected. "Do we have to drive?" She inhaled the hint of salt in the air.

"Most people take transportation in San Francisco."

"Why?"

"Just city practice, I guess. And the hills can be

daunting."

"I'm in shape for it… Are you?" She noted how his expression narrowed after he glanced at her sandals.

"I'm in shape for just about anything you care to throw at me. Just how functional are you in those heels?"

"These aren't heels." She lifted one foot to emphasize the fact. She dropped her leg when he grinned.

"They're sandals with a one-inch rise. Easy walking shoes." She groaned under her breath. Could she get used to this pretence? Since he was such a talented actor, why didn't he just play up his nice persona for the media? He wouldn't need a fake girlfriend then. Something about this girlfriend scenario escaped her—she didn't quite understand. Yet.

"Okay, but, only if you're sure you won't get blisters."

"Positive."

He waved the limo off and extended his hand.

She hesitated.

The spark of a dare lit behind his eyes.

She had no doubt, if she didn't co-operate, he'd start kissing her for all of San Francisco to see. She'd had all the physical contact she could handle for one day. Blowing out a slow breath, she held out her hand, and his fingers threaded through hers. They must portray a happy couple for whoever cared to glance their way as they sauntered along the sidewalk. That thought curdled in her stomach. A niggling reminder, all wasn't what it seemed when the papers printed stories about billionaires. She tried to extricate her hand twice.

But he didn't let her go.

She slowed outside a store window to admire a purse.

Cole stopped and waited.

His patience she wouldn't have expected. Not something Rodney would ever have done. Kate sneaked a glance at Cole's image in the reflection. He was so different from Rodney. Cole was tall with thick brown hair and intelligent brown eyes. He didn't exactly dress to impress, but he looked good in what he wore.

Rodney, on the other hand, had been much shorter, with dirty blond hair and added streaks. And rather than intelligent, Rodney's eyes were small and greedy. Why hadn't she realized that before he'd thrown her under the bus?

"Nice purse." In a competition, Cole would win hands down. She used the moment to drive the comparisons between the two men out of her mind.

"Very nice."

She leaned closer. She couldn't read the tag, but when she tilted her head just a little, she gasped at the price. *Six thousand dollars*! "Maybe not that pretty." She didn't want her lack of funds to be so obvious. The last thing she wanted was for him to think she'd been hinting for the billionaire to buy her an extravagant purse. He already thought she was doing this for money. Heaven forbid.

When they arrived at the wharf, even though the sun shone overhead, she saw low-lying fog creep along the water, draping the bay in a moody atmosphere. An occasional breeze blew in their direction, and the fog carried a draft of cool air. She shivered.

"Cold?" he asked.

"No, I'm fine." She rubbed the goose bumps on her arms. She should've remembered to carry a sweater in case it got cool near the water.

"I'm glad you suggested we walk." He smiled and wrapped an arm around her shoulders. "It's nice to get out and stretch my legs, now and then."

"I can't see any signs of paparazzi." She silently thanked him for the warmth of his arm.

"So far." He cast a serious glance around. "At least, none we can see."

"Oh." She hadn't considered that. She glanced around.

"As long as we play the happy couple, we don't have to worry about paparazzi."

Not sure that was true. *How would she manage being alone in San Francisco with Cole?*

For one thing, she didn't do downtime. She didn't take vacations or visit expensive restaurants. She worked day-in-and-day-out alongside her employees.

She glanced at Cole. Did he ever do manual labor? He'd been born rich. Had he ever known a moment of uncertainty in business? "I'm curious. How'd you get us in ahead of the line?" She turned in her seat to peruse the crowed room, before putting her napkin on her lap.

He winked and seated himself next to her. "I have my ways."

Good thing she bit back her feelings about rich people getting special treatment, because she remembered he'd said he'd booked the reservation yesterday. He hadn't tried to pay their way inside tonight. She'd just expected the worst from him. She couldn't spend the next few days despising everything he did. She'd be civil, and maybe the next few days wouldn't be as bad.

Her plan worked, and they chatted about everyday things while they waited for their meal.

Cole listened to what she said and commented whenever appropriate. He laughed a few times.

She did, too. It all felt so scripted and fake. Halfway through the meal, she realized Cole hadn't once made her feel as if she'd bored him. Another thing Rodney had done all the time. Why had she ever loved him?

After dinner, Cole extracted his cell phone, then hesitated. "I was about to call for the limo, but we can walk back if you want to?"

"Yes, please, I've never been here before, and it's such a nice evening."

After leaving Pier Twenty-One, they sauntered along the sidewalk. The fog was gone, and the warmth had returned. She followed the sound of nearby music, not knowing if they were walking in the direction of their hotel. "Do you think it's a club?"

"I think so." Cole looked at the sign over the door.

A long line of people zigzagged down the sidewalk, waiting to get inside.

"Maybe it's just for club members." If things were different, she'd have loved to check it out.

"One way to find out." He strode past the line and stepped up to the doorman. "Any chance of getting inside tonight?"

"Maybe," the doorman said, eyeing Cole's expensive watch.

Cole slipped him a bill, and they got entrance without question.

"Under normal circumstances, I'd object to what

you just did. But I have the feeling this is the norm for clubs like this one."

He nodded.

Packed inside, bodies writhed to the rhythm of familiar music. A live band performed on the tiny stage.

"It's Breach!" she shouted to be heard over the music. "How did a small club like this get a band this big?"

"I see a free table. Hurry, before we lose it." Cole grabbed Kate's hand and pulled her through the crowd.

A server stopped at their table. "What can I get you folks?"

"How'd you get Breach to play here?" Kate asked, after they ordered drinks.

"They got their first gig here, and they come back once a year to reconnect with their base." The server left to get their order.

"That's quite a coup for this establishment." She leaned forward to get a good look at the band members.

"Yeah, but we all have to start somewhere, and it's nice they appreciate the people who gave them their opportunity." Cole glanced around, but not at the band.

Kate had noted his vigilance earlier. A flash exploded from across the room.

He twisted his head to the left. "Uh-oh!"

Kate spotted the camera just as Cole grabbed her hand again. "It seems our evening will be ruined by the underbelly of the press."

"Oh, no!" She pursed her lips. "Can't we stay? Do we have to leave?"

Chapter Seven

Cole hated himself for believing they could enter the club and enjoy a few moments together. For the first time since he'd coerced her to do this, she seemed to enjoy herself, and he liked it when she smiled. He hated that the paparazzi had found them, even though being found and photographed was the point. "We'd better go."

"No. Let's stay." She didn't budge from her chair.

"They'll take pictures the whole time we're here." He leaned closer to speak over the music.

Kate whipped her sunglasses out of her purse. "Now I know why movie stars always have sunglasses on. Those flashes are hard on the eyes when they go off ten or twenty at a time. I'm seeing stars and not the exciting kind."

He raised his hands in surrender. "Okay, just remember, I warned you."

Their drinks arrived, and she took a sip of her mojito. "Let's stay, at least for a little while. I've never seen Breach live."

Cole leaned back in his chair but felt every bunched muscle in his back. She didn't know how difficult this could get. Worse, they didn't have a vehicle to jump into to escape the paparazzi.

Before long, a swarm of paparazzi had gathered near the door.

If Kate imagined she'd be able to make it back to the hotel on foot, she'd be disappointed.

A tall man with a deep scar across his cheek approached. "Mr. Prentice, I'm very sorry to have to ask you to leave. It's unfortunate, but the band is our claim to fame, and they create the best business of our year." He shoved some cards into Cole's hand. "Please come back tomorrow or whenever you can, and we'll make it up to you."

As Cole suspected, they were taking attention away from the band, and the management didn't want them to be overshadowed. He eyed Kate and shrugged. "Not a problem. I'll just call my limo." He already had his cell phone in his hand. They couldn't have stayed much longer, anyway. Cole noted Kate's shrug, but said nothing within earshot of the proprietor.

When she touched his hand, another spate of camera flashes blinded them.

"I don't understand. We've done nothing. Why doesn't the management make the paparazzi leave?"

"Because Breach put the club on the map. They want the band to be showcased and featured in the papers tomorrow." He took a last sip of his drink, enjoying the spiced flavor with a hint of mint. He set his glass down and surveyed the room. The crowd, wrapped up in the sensory explosion of music and lights, didn't notice the paparazzi's intrusion. "They're smart enough to realize we might take the headline away." He received a text indicating the limo was outside. He stood and wrapped one arm around Kate's right shoulder to lead her out of the club.

A reporter moved in like a tiger shark—eyes rolled back. He chased them through the crowd toward the door.

"Miss, Miss. Have you been dating Cole Prentice long?" A mic shoved into her face, grazing past her.

Cole yanked her back.

"We've been dating for a week," she said while walking away.

But the paparazzo followed.

"And you're already on vacation together," the paparazzo said, waggling his eyebrows.

Seeing her mouth open, Cole gave her shoulders a gentle squeeze. "Don't react," he said close to her ear. "That's what they want." Cole hated this part. He hated to see the air of desperation in anyone who dared to get close, coerced or not. "No comment." Cole threaded his fingers with hers, then pulled her through the throng of partiers. Crowded by the paparazzi near the front door, he placed her in front of him and kept his arm around her to protect her as best he could.

Initially, he'd been so angry about being duped, he hadn't cared about her feelings. But seeing how vulnerable she was in this situation, he hated what he'd done. He'd forced her into this.

He didn't have a choice; he had to continue with the charade—for the company's sake and because the board demanded he provide a more stable private life to assuage shareholders' fears that his lifestyle and bad publicity had become problematic for the company.

"They'll get the wrong idea about us." Kate yanked her arm out of his grasp as soon as they got outside. "Why didn't you tell him we're in separate rooms?"

Cole glimpsed over his shoulder to see if anyone had followed them yet. His jaw tensed. The white limo arrived, and he yanked the door open. "Isn't that the main idea? To create a buzz between us? Get in."

She opened her mouth, no doubt to object, before she spotted photographers dashing after them. She jumped in and edged over to make room for Cole.

Two more flashes blinded them before they got away.

"Answer me, darn it. Why didn't you set the man straight?" She scowled at Cole.

Cole's jaw bunched, and he frowned. "Because, no matter what you tell them, they write whatever sells papers. Do you think they'd believe we have separate hotel rooms?" He made an exasperated sound. "Even my friends wouldn't believe that." Clenching the door handle, he stared out the window, watching the buildings go by without seeing them.

This trip might be more stressful than he expected. He didn't intend to care about Kate's feelings. So why did he? How had she managed to change the way he felt about her? Had she tricked him again?

Chapter Eight

When Kate's alarm rang the next morning, she woke to sunlight filtering through the curtains. She moaned and stuck out a floundering hand to hit the button on the clock.

Nothing happened. The ringing continued.

She forced one eye open, realizing it was the phone, not the clock. A low groan—oh right, she wasn't at home. "Go away." She buried her face in the pillow. It continued ringing, so she picked it up and slammed it down on the cradle again without answering. Silence. She smiled.

The silence didn't last long; the phone started ringing again. She ignored it, and then knocking began on the door between the two adjoining rooms.

"Kate, you okay in there?"

Mother of God! "I'm sleeping! Go away," she shouted. The phone started ringing again.

"It's not me on the phone," he said through the door.

Kate rolled over in bed and grappled with the handset. "Hello?"

"You not up yet?"

Cole's voice held humor she didn't appreciate. "You said you weren't phoning me."

"Yeah, sorry about that. I lied."

She groaned into the phone. "What time is it?"

"Six o'clock."

"Six o'clock! You're kidding! Why are you up at this time of the morning when we're on holiday? And why in blazes are you waking me up, too?"

"If we want to evade the paparazzi, we'll have to leave before they're up and around."

She sighed and raked her fingers through her messy hair, frowning at the door between their two rooms. "Who said I want to do that?"

"This is my first vacation in years, remember? I've rented a hot air balloon ride in Napa Valley. Then we'll go on a tour of some vineyards, do some wine tasting, have a nice dinner, etc."

"Hot air ballooning before breakfast?" Since she had a terrible fear of heights, she pressed her hand against a lump of clay forming in her stomach and threatening to fill her whole chest. No way would she tell him something he could use against her.

"We'll go for breakfast on the way. You up for it, Ms. Cameron, or do I go alone and hope the paparazzi doesn't show up to find me alone?"

Had there been a veiled threat in his statement? If they had a public fight, wouldn't it be better? "Uh, maybe it would get us both off the hook if they thought we had an argument. Then I can go home."

"That can't happen. And you'll be in breach of your promise to me."

He'd switched to a formal tone, making her feel guilty. Moments ago, he'd sounded almost carefree. She propped herself up on one arm and frowned at the closed door between their rooms. She pictured him on the other side, dressed and ready to go—no doubt, showered, shaved, and smelling very masculine. "I need a shower, give me twenty minutes." She sat up on the side of the bed and imagined she could feel his grin through the phone line.

Taking the quickest shower possible, she left her hair damp and threw on a pair of lightweight beige capris and sleeveless peach blouse. This time she brought a lightweight peach sweater. She also stuffed some suntan lotion and the hotel's complimentary bottle of water and an apple in her purse. She was ready at six thirty. Rather than phone him, she knocked on the door between their two rooms.

"It's open," he called.

She cracked open the door and peered inside.

Laying down a hairbrush, he smiled.

His hair had a more tousled appearance this morning, making it soft and springy and hugging the curves of his ears. Dressed in khaki shorts and a beige T-shirt, he projected himself as a normal guy. A normal hot-hunky calendar type of guy—darn it. He appeared happy and relaxed, and with a camera slung around his neck, he was all tourist today.

He glanced at his watch. "I can't believe you got ready so fast."

"You've been hanging around with too many prima donnas." Given the hot air balloon trip, she forced the memory of their upcoming day's adventure out of her terrified thoughts. Somehow, she'd have to get out of the balloon ride before it happened.

He rubbed his hands together, then motioned to his main door. "Let's get going." At the bottom of the stairs, he held the door and led her to a low-slung red convertible in the parking garage.

Running a hand over her long hair, she cringed. It

would be a tangled mess after riding in a convertible. Then she remembered she had an elastic in her purse. "No chauffeur today?" She dug in her purse, then snapped her hair into a ponytail.

"Nope, it's just the two of us, and a hot air balloon soaring over the valley."

She felt sick at the thought.

"The balloon ride is a couple of hours from here." He smiled as they got back into the convertible after stopping for breakfast as a small diner. "There'll be some nice scenery on the way."

Little did he know, his information did nothing to ease her anxiety. They arrived at the balloon ride just before eleven o'clock. A massive orange-and-blue striped balloon floated in the field, tugging at its tethers, and seeming to be in a hurry to meet the sky.

Kate's insides roiled, while moisture formed on her brow—she just might be sick.

Cole parked the convertible and killed the ignition. He faced Kate, grinning like a kid. "You ready for this adventure?"

"Uh, Cole, you need to know something about me." She grasped her chest.

A shadow flitted across his face. "What is it?"

"I'm afraid of heights. I can't go up in that balloon." She had a death grip on the door handle with one hand and her shirt with the other. The confession of her deepest fear hadn't worked the way she'd hoped. She expected he at least might get ticked off and go without her.

Instead, he focused on her and smiled.

Oh heck, no...he had the appearance of a man who wanted to help a gal get over her fear. *Nuh uh! She didn't want any of that.* She opened her door, got out, and frowned at him. "No. No. No. Don't even think about it." She pressed herself against the car. "I can't."

He held his palms out, moving closer. "You can, you know. This is a perfect time for you to try it. It's as safe as riding in this vehicle on the highway."

She didn't believe it for a second. "Doesn't matter. I'll get dizzy. I'll throw up in the basket. That'll ruin your fun and everyone else's." *Not to mention my own.* She couldn't quell her juddering nerves.

"That's okay. I'll go by myself." His shoulders slumped, and he pulled a ticket out of his pocket. "Some people can't take certain kinds of risks in life. This is one of them for you. I understand that. I don't want to pressure you if you're not ready."

She hadn't expected him to cave—or be quite so understanding. She surveyed everything but the balloon. "Thank you."

"You can wait here in the car. Too bad, you don't have a book or something. The flight itself is an hour. We land down for dinner before returning. The entire process takes three or four hours, I believe." He got out of the vehicle and stared up at the multicolored balloon, then toward her. "No, I can't leave you here for that long. We could leave. I'm sorry I didn't check with you before we came. Just because I'm excited about the trip, I shouldn't have assumed you would be too."

"Yes, you can go. I'm all grown up, and…I have lots of books on my phone app. I have a bottle of water in my purse, and I even packed an apple for a snack. I'll be fine until you get back."

He stared at the balloon for a minute. "No, it's too long."

He sounded hopeful she'd change her mind. Or was it her imagination? Her stomach hollowed out, and she bent over, just slightly. Had he guilted her into going? If so, it ticked her off.

Every time she glanced at the balloon, the earth became less firm under her feet. Hinting she was up to accepting challenges within her comfort zone was unfair.

Still, sweat beaded her forehead while she forced herself to take a step toward the balloon. If he'd done this on purpose to get her into such a rickety basket, then she'd make him sorry for it later. But for now, she couldn't let him prove her unworthy of a challenge. For her own self-respect, she straightened her shoulders, even while her stomach gurgled, and she took a deep breath. "I'll need an anti-nauseant." She breathed in and out in a controlled way.

"Excuse me, Miss? I have some right here."A stranger approached from the parking lot.

She hadn't noticed him until he spoke. She smiled at him. "Uh, thank you, no."

"It's okay. If you're taking the balloon ride, I'd prefer anyone who even suspects nausea, take this first. It's chewable and fast-acting." He held out a packet with foil-wrapped pills. "I'm the gondolier. You'll be going up with me today."

"Will taking these pills be between us? You won't tell anyone you've given this to me?"

"As a gentleman, I would never," the older man said. His gray bushy mustache wiggled when he smiled. "Name's Jake, by the way."

"Nice to meet you, Jake. I'm Kate, and thanks. I hope they work fast enough." She popped two orange pills into her mouth, chewed, and swallowed.

"They will. I'll have to go over safety measures, etc., before we lift off. You'll have plenty of time to settle your tummy first."

"I appreciate it."

Cole handed her a bottle of water.

She took a long sip to get the taste of the pills out of her mouth. "Thanks."

The gondolier considered her nice leather sandals. "I appreciate you agreed to take the pills." He winked. "We wouldn't want to ruin your new shoes."

"I can tell you've had experience with other nervous fliers."

He laughed and rubbed his mustache between his fingers. "It's surprising how many people do this to combat their fear of heights."

"Does it often work?" Her stomach tightened.

"For some it does." Jake smiled again. "I can tell it will for you."

"I hope you're right." Kate appreciated Cole's patience, giving her the chance to decide before they neared the balloon. *Someday, her stubbornness would kill her. Literally.* She noted Cole appeared ten years younger today, as if all his stresses were gone at this moment. She hoped she didn't panic in the air and ruin it all for him.

When they reached the basket, he took her in. "You're sure? You don't have to come."

He was wrong. She didn't have a choice. This was part of the bargain, wasn't it? What Rosa was being paid for. "Wouldn't want you to have all the fun without me." Even though she'd tried, she'd failed to sound confident.

The other young woman in the basket giggled while staring into her boyfriend's eyes.

Seeing such happiness drew Kate out of her own misery. Nice to see a young couple in love. It meant there might be hope for her someday. Climbing into the basket made her legs feel weak. They didn't want to cooperate, so Cole helped to hoist her in. Her breathing had become fast and shallow, but the anti-nauseants were working so far.

While the last checks were being made, the basket wobbled with disconcerting regularity.

Cole's left arm circled her shoulders, and he leaned nearer. "You can still back out. You don't have to prove anything to me."

She didn't meet his gaze. "I'm proving it to myself," she lied.

He squeezed her shoulders a little tighter. "Good girl."

Kate hated when his words of praise hit home. Still, if she could get over this fear, maybe she could get past other things that held her back, too. Tick it off her bucket list.

Chapter Nine

When the gondola lifted off the ground, Cole reprimanded himself internally. Kate must really think him a jerk, now. Had he forced her into this? He'd never seen a person turn so white, so fast. He kept his arm around her shoulders, if for no other reason than to keep her from falling to the floor of the craft.

The other couple held hands and stared into each other's eyes. The beautiful views of vineyards below were lost to them. Evident to everyone in the gondola, they were already high on love.

His inner cynicism had kicked into gear.

When they ascended to soar across the vineyards, a bird flew by. A beautiful hawk. The creature stared as if they were invading his territory. Well, they were.

Kate gasped, and her violet eyes opened a little wider. "Did you see that magnificent creature?"

Her words clung like static, because the beauty he experienced right now was her. He loosened his grip when her trembling lessened, and a little color returned to her cheeks.

"The hawk's talons were much bigger than I imagined." She grabbed the side of the basket when it wobbled in a breeze.

"I didn't notice. I noticed its magnificent head, those intelligent eyes, and the strength of its body."

She tugged away. Was she ready? He let her make

her own decision. He didn't want to set her back to her trembling state. By the time they touched down, she appeared to be stronger. Happier than he'd seen her since they met. Unless he missed his guess, she liked the thrill of her accomplishment today, and who could blame her? Fear of heights was no small matter. She'd taken a gigantic step.

Later that evening, they arrived at the hotel still on a high from their day in the sunshine. They'd visited several vineyards and tasted wine, but since he was driving, he stopped at a couple of sips.

The paparazzi didn't find them, making the day even better.

They strolled through the lobby without a care. "Hungry?" he asked.

"Ravenous." She laughed.

Note to self, wine makes her giggle. He grinned and stabbed the elevator button. "Let's shower and get dressed and meet in the lobby for dinner, shall we?" He lifted an arm and checked his watch. "Say about eight p.m.?"

"Dare we?"

"I've spoken to the hotel management, and they've promised to keep the paparazzi out."

"It's a date." She smiled.

Her previous paleness had been sun-kissed today, and she exuded a glow. Would there have been this kind of chemistry between them if they'd met without deception—and the lure of his money?

Twenty minutes later, waiting in the lobby near the elevators, Cole held the door at eight p.m. on the dot. Seeing her hesitate as she returned his gaze elevated his pulse. She could rev him up or shut him down with a mere glance. But tonight—the message in her eyes—was he misreading it? Had she softened toward him?

After he stabbed the elevator button for the second floor restaurant, the doors slid shut with them inside. He admired her poise. She wore a sleeveless turquoise dress with matching heels and clutch. She exuded confidence and beauty in everything she wore. She made everything look expensive.

Their gazes met, and his heart pumped a little harder—no mistaking the message in her eyes. He touched her hand.

She lifted her face to his.

And man. When he tasted her, he lost all sanity. He'd never experienced anything like this when kissing a woman. She was like ambrosia. Her scent mingled with sunscreen and fresh air.

The headiest aroma he could imagine.

While he was enjoying the kiss, he assumed she'd shove him away at any moment or the elevator door would open, so he groped around until he found the elevator stop button. The alarm bell rang for a few seconds.

Then she found the button, forcing the elevator to continue on its way.

Her gorgeous eyes drew him in. He leaned down to kiss her again, just as the elevator stopped, and the doors opened on the third floor for more guests to enter.

Kate gasped and flattened a firm hand on his chest.

At first, he believed Kate's reaction had been embarrassment, until he noted her expression had become sharp and wounded.

She sank against his side and grabbed his hand as if it were a lifeline.

What was going on?

The woman who'd entered the elevator covered a grin with her hand at catching them, while the man glared at Cole.

Kate didn't utter a word.

If Cole wasn't imagining it, she had become pale again.

"Kate, how have you been?"

He didn't take his gaze off her. That's when the woman changed from a smile to a cautious re-examination of the situation. Cole frowned. Kate was acquainted with this man. That might explain her instant withdrawal and change of attitude. Just by the way she reacted, Cole wanted to punch this guy's clock.

"Fine, thank you." She stared straight ahead.

"Won't you introduce us?"

Silence. Cole guessed she had no intention of doing it.

"Well, I'll do the honors."

He sounded as if his introduction was a chore.

"I'm Rodney Hollander, and this is Karina Vaughan-Hollander, my wife. We got married today. Maybe you already knew that?"

Cole noted the satisfied reaction on the man's face in front of him, as if he'd done more than make introductions. He'd done it to hurt Kate. Lightbulb moment. Rodney Hollander. Cole had read about Hollander's breakup with Kate, but he didn't believe what the media had said. Well versed in how articles were written about him, Cole found the article saying Kate was a gold digger difficult to believe.

"Have we met?" The woman eyed her up and down.

"Hello, Karina." Her voice wavered. "My name is Kate, Kate Cameron."

Two bright spots appeared on Karina Vaughan's face. "Oh, I see. I didn't realize. What are you doing in San Francisco?"

Somehow, her tone had gone from collected to jealous in a second. Cole examined the ex-fiancé. So, this was the guy who'd left Kate for another woman. His clothes were expensive, and the woman's attire brand name all the way. He'd spotted the enormous diamonds on her ring finger, all shiny and new.

"Wait a minute." Hollander shook a finger at Cole, and his smile widened.

Cole gritted his teeth. Hollander had two seconds to get out of his face.

"You're Cole Prentice, aren't you?"

"I am." Cole used his best billionaire tone to shut the guy down.

"We met at the Byzantine Club a few years ago at a fundraiser." Hollander made a sound between his tongue and teeth while his gaze strayed to Kate. "Maybe that's where you met Kate?"

Cole frowned. "No, we didn't meet there." He fisted his hand when the idiot intimated Kate had been seeing him while engaged to Hollander. Kate had gone paler than she'd been in the gondola. Cole grabbed Kate's hand before the elevator doors closed and pulled her out onto the third floor.

Meanwhile, Rodney Hollander was taking an ear-lashing from his bride, even before the elevator doors closed again.

Chapter Ten

Rodney Hollander and his new bride were in San Francisco at the same time. How could fate be so cruel? She never wanted to see the man again, but news of his marriage had been all over the papers. He'd married Karina Vaughan, heiress to Vaughan Steel. Karina was daddy's little girl, and her father had blessed the union by buying them an immense mansion as a wedding gift.

Kate had put the pain behind her until seeing Rodney in the elevator. Wrenching every embarrassing, heartbreaking moment back. In fact, back then, Kate believed nothing had been wrong between her and Rodney, until the news of his engagement to Karina Vaughan hit the papers—while he'd still been engaged to her.

The front pages had been all about Rodney and the millionaire heiress he was dating. Photos had been splashed everywhere. To Kate's ultimate embarrassment and shock, most of her friends had pitied her.

And, as if that hadn't been bad enough, Rodney had laughed when she'd confronted him. He'd taunted her by asking if she believed he could marry someone who'd grown up in foster care? Someone who didn't even know her parents' history.

Kate didn't hate Ms. Vaughan for stealing her fiancé. She had empathy for the woman. Karina was a somewhat plain, non-adventurous multi-millionaire's daughter, who seemed awkward in public. Their engagement lasted so long before marriage, Kate figured Karina's father insisted on a decent engagement period. Rodney would have wanted to close the deal before Karina could change her mind.

Of course, Kate regretted that she had ever loved Rodney and had wanted a forever after. She'd been blinded by love. His betrayal forced her to understand his many shortcomings and his selfishness during their relationship. She shouldn't have been so blind. Everything always had to be his way. Money was his holy grail. Not his love for her, or anyone else.

Rodney never would have stayed. Even though he had a couple of million dollars of his own, left by his philanthropist father, Rodney wanted the power only old money could garner. His father had made money on the stock market in the seventies. Being nouveau riche didn't hold the same cache for Rodney. Marrying into the Vaughn family had been the way to get old money status.

"How in blazes did he end up here?"

Cole's voice pulled Kate out of her reverie. She had the distinct feeling Cole had done his homework about herself and Rodney. Had it been in the write-up Rosa had given him? No, Rosa wouldn't do that. She didn't blame Cole for checking her out. She did the same thing by going online and finding every article she could. "I didn't know he'd be here. He has nothing to do with me anymore." At the sound of her voice cracking, she gritted her teeth.

Cole sighed. "Didn't seem that way in the elevator. Do you still care for him?"

Kate squeezed one hand to her stomach. "No!"

"If you say so."

Cole sounded skeptical. "I'm not feeling well. You realize we exited the elevator on the wrong floor, don't you?"

"Yes, I just wanted to get you out of there before you lost all color in your face."

"I did not."

"I'm afraid you did."

"Don't tell me you didn't already know about Rodney and me. I'm sure you read the muck the papers printed back then." She planted her arms over her chest. "And, if you think he and I had an affair while he was dating his wonderful Karina, you're wrong. It was the other way around." Kate marched down the hall toward the stairs.

Cole followed.

She wrenched open the door and began up the stairs. She'd almost escaped into her room when he touched her arm.

"Kate, talk to me."

She started walking. "I...I don't want to."

"Do you still love him?"

Blinking hard against tears, she hated the way Cole gazed into her eyes, as if to gauge the truth of her reply. "I already told you, no."

"Tell me why you're so upset, then."

Kate slid the key card into the slot, even though her hands were vibrating. The lock changed to green, and she cracked the door. Memories of Cole's kiss in the elevator sent her senses into an uproar. She needed to regain her perspective. But first, she needed to call Rosa and resign her assignment.

What tempted her to even consider falling for another rich man? Seeing Rodney reminded her why she'd never allow herself to be duped again. Never again.

Rodney had been a much-needed dash of cold water. She sighed. The fact stood, she couldn't go backward. And, right now, she didn't want to talk—to anyone—especially with Cole. "I'm tired, Cole. Discussing Rodney Hollander is off the table. Go to bed. We've had a long day." She ran a hand over her eyes.

"But we're having dinner," he reminded.

"I'm not hungry anymore. Please have dinner by yourself tonight." She stepped inside, closed the door, and leaned against it. Bombarded by too many sensory overloads today, she needed some downtime. The whole thing had been more than she could handle.

To his benefit, Cole wanted to know her version of what had happened between her and Rodney. She couldn't tell him. After all, he was a client, not someone she could trust. And she couldn't forget he was no better, since he'd blackmailed her to be here.

Maybe Rodney had done her a favor by reminding her men like him wanted rich women with a pedigree, and she was Cole's hired plaything. She yanked out her suitcase and started stuffing clothes and toiletries into the bag. Rosa would just have to come up with another solution, because Kate couldn't do this to herself any longer.

Two hours later, after pacing back and forth, and unable to come up with a solution, she rubbed her tense shoulders. She dropped into a chair. Finding a solution was hopeless.

She'd heard Cole return to his room half an hour ago. For several minutes, Kate dreaded a knock on her door. Thank heavens, it didn't happen. Finally, she'd decided. She opened her door and let it snick closed with little noise. Suitcase in hand, she hit the elevator button and stepped inside. An unexpected hand poked through to stop the doors from closing.

Rodney swaggered into the elevator.

The smell of alcohol filled the small pace.

"Fancy meeting you here again," he slurred.

Kate noted his dirty blond, highlighted hair was a mess, as if he'd been leaning on the bar and running his fingers through it. "You, again." She kept her voice disinterested, while holding her suitcase handle in a vise grip. His room was on the third floor, not the fifth. What was he doing here? *Waiting for her?*

"Yeah," he sneered. "Should've been a good night, but you ruined everything by showing up here on my honeymoon—and with your gigolo, no less. My wealthy, irritated bride is taking her jealousy out on me, as if it's my fault you and I have a lusty past. How is it you showed up at our hotel—tonight of all nights? How can you afford a place like this, anyway?" He touched a finger to the side of his nose. "Wait, I know. You're using another rich man to get ahead."

Until now, Kate might not have understood the term, seeing red. Her blood pressure spiked. "You chased me! Not the other way around. My biggest regret is that I didn't see through you sooner. I nearly lost my business because you left me holding the tab for the wedding venue."

Rodney chuckled. "Coming from poverty, I'm sure you would have survived if you'd had to claim bankruptcy."

"You self-serving clod!" Kate wanted to slap his face, but she wouldn't give him the chance to charge her with assault.

"Karina thinks you're here on purpose because you couldn't bear me marrying her." He staggered for a second and pitched a little closer.

The smell of booze grew, and she glanced up at the floor indicator lights. They were on the fourth floor. The elevators were slow tonight.

"She thinks you want me back."

He grinned like an idiot. "Like that would happen." Kate gritted her teeth. "Does she know she was sleeping with you when we were engaged?"

He winked, and a sly grin appeared.

Jerk. Her gut twisted.

"Well, maybe I'm sorry you and I split up." He fondled her hair. "Maybe I made a mistake."

She shoved his hand away. "Get your paws off me, Rodney. You're despicable." In hindsight, maybe she should thank the new Mrs. Hollander for saving her from making another mistake with Cole.

Rodney's expression darkened, reminding Kate he could get cranky when he was drinking. She crowded into the far side of the elevator and hoped he'd get the message. He dove forward and pinned her into the corner. His boozy breath and slack body invaded her personal space.

He hadn't touched her—yet. But his actions led her to believe he would. Experience told her he was an unstable drunk, and that made her edgy.

Within seconds, his hands were on her shoulders. She'd tried to shove him off but didn't have the strength against his drunken deadweight and body size. She heard someone enter the elevator before a hand grabbed the back of his shirt and flung him into the hall.

He landed on his rear end with an "oomph."

Cole turned to her and narrowed his gaze. "Are you okay?"

Rodney got up, wobbling a bit.

His angry expression led her to believe he might try to take Cole on.

Cole frowned at him. "Don't even consider it, buddy. I'm an experienced fighter, and I'm sober. You'd lose."

Rodney staggered sideways and tried to purse his flaccid lips in reaction to Cole's warning. Inebriated or not, the threat worked, and he dropped his fists and backed down. "She's after your money, buddy." He puffed up his chest. "She'll do anything to hook her claws into someone with dough."

"You are a liar, Rodney." The words came out in a whisper, her throat tight with emotion.

He laughed. His facial features drooped, while he squinted at them. "Can you prove it?"

She clenched her hands. She bit her tongue.

Rodney gave up and wandered off.

Maybe because Cole's murderous expression scared him. She hoped so. The second he'd left, Kate edged past Cole and headed for the front door of the hotel.

Chapter Eleven

The lobby of the hotel had been buzzing with activity but fell silent the instant she burst out of the elevator with suitcase in hand.

Cole followed close behind. "Where do you think you're going?"

"I've had all I can take. It doesn't matter what you threaten me with, Cole Prentice, this pretence is over. I can't go through this." She glanced over her shoulder. "I'm sorry."

"It's over when I say it's over." With a gentle hand, he drew her toward a fountain in the center of the lobby.

She sat on the edge of the fountain. When his muscled thigh rubbed against her bare leg, she wished she had worn jeans rather than shorts. They'd already caught the attention of too many people in the lobby. It seemed everyone stared at them. "To be honest, I've had it with men like you and Rodney. I want to go home." She pressed her arms over her chest. She didn't care that he avoided meeting her gaze while muscles worked in his jaw.

"Please, don't put me in the same category as Hollander. I'm not like him. Not at all."

"Aren't you?" Kate's voice caught against her will. "If you're not like him, then let me go home."

He observed her, his gaze softening. "I'm not like

him. That's why I can't let you go. You and I have a deal. I haven't tried to trick you, Kate. I've laid my truth on the table. With no deception on my part—I'm afraid you'll just have to go along with my plan or pay the consequences."

He sounded tired and less menacing than the first time he'd threatened her with ruination. She wouldn't blame him if he believed she was a fortune hunter. Many people believed the media after Rodney's tirade and the articles in the newspapers at the time of their breakup.

Right now, she didn't care what he believed. She glanced at the lobby's revolving doors, spinning like a beckoning escape route. "I'm leaving." She jumped up, grabbed her suitcase, and headed for the exit.

He followed close on her heels. "Don't step outside those doors, Kate. If you want everything to be back to normal, heed my warning."

She ignored him and continued her path to freedom. As far as she was concerned, she'd done her job.

"Kate, listen to me." He strolled alongside her.

Ignoring him, she made it through the revolving door and raised her right arm to hail a taxi. Flashing lights blinded her. Her heart squeezed. Holding a hand over her eyes to block the flashes, she turned toward the hotel, again to see Cole waiting inside. He didn't appear angry, just tired. She mouthed his name.

One of the more aggressive photogs tried to get right in her face.

Cole rushed to her rescue.

Relief filled her when Cole's broad shoulders blocked the flashing cameras. She peered around him, only to be blinded again. Using her better judgment, she dove for the cover of his arm.

He leaned down. "I tried to warn you. If you leave like this, the media will hound you for ages. They'll want to know what happened between us. And your life will be miserable. Trust me."

"Okay, I understand why you tried to warn me. Hurry, let's get back inside."

Cole led her to a less-populated area. "Let's talk here." He pointed to two chairs in a quiet corner. "I'm curious. Why were you running away now? I thought things were going well."

"You believe what Rodney said about me, don't you?" She scowled, then looked away. *Why did it matter what he believed?*

He paused.

Too long.

"What if I do? This thing between us isn't real, Kate. None of it. We're in a contract, you and I. We don't care a whit about what either of us thinks about the other—do we?"

She heaved a sigh and tilted her head. "And you can live with the fact that I'm such a conniving fortune hunter?"

"I think so." He rubbed the back of his neck. "Not to offend you, but I wasn't about to hand you my grandmother's diamond ring or anything. I rarely go into a contract without doing my due diligence, I knew about your history with Hollander, and I ignored it."

She cringed. No doubt, Cole mentioned the ring because Rodney had given her his grandmother's diamond, until Karina, then he'd wanted it back. "You're wrong about me, Mr. Prentice." She braced her hands on the arms of the chair and leaned forward. "I'm attempting to help you. I am not using deception." She paused. "At least, not in the way you think."

"Let's go back to our room before the paparazzi get inside."

Nodding, she slowly pushed to her feet.

Cole picked up her suitcase. "Kate, if we do this thing, it'll be over before you know it."

"I'm not sure it's the right thing for me." But she wanted to help Rosa.

He exhaled. "I didn't want to have to say this again, but you have obligated yourself to carry through with the contract. If you renege, you know what'll happen. I guarantee you won't like it."

She bit her lip. *How could she have kissed him and meant it?*

"For now, until Rosa finds a loophole to get me out of this mess. After that, our deal ends." She shifted another glance toward the throng of photographers outside the hotel windows. "Another thing you should know—I don't like you, Cole Prentice, and I think you are keeping something from me. Something to do with why you're blackmailing me into staying on."

He grinned. "I thought we agreed on a solution? Anyway, as you can see, I'm not in the least dinged by your comment. I know where I stand with you. It makes our arrangement so much easier."

His words held a hint of bitterness.

Before the elevator doors closed, he tipped her chin with two fingers and squashed his hot lips onto hers. Lights flashed through the hotel window, and the lobby grew silent.

"It's unfortunate this little escapade has created too

much media buzz. Our next few days will be even more uncomfortable, because I'll have to prove you are the love of my life, and I'm not about to let you go. So, get ready for the ride, sweet cakes. It's about to get rocky."

She hated the way he'd called her sweet cakes with his condescending tone of voice. "I have no choice?" Her throat constricted, and she blinked back tears. Why was he so desperate to keep her on as his girlfriend? Another reason than the one he'd told her had to exist.

He caressed her upper arm, then his fingers drifted to her chin, and he tipped her head up again. "You have a choice. But what just happened outside is small potatoes to what you'll experience if we don't end our so-called relationship in a proper way. In public, you'll have to kiss me and pretend to like it." He smiled and gazed into her eyes as if she meant the world. "They're still watching."

"You are such a…!"

He laughed for real then. "Now you're getting it. My company is at stake. I'm not about to let you ruin that. I don't care if you hightail it with that bozo Hollander when this is over. But you'll carry out your obligation to me first. He can't outdistance me."

Kate's internal four-year-old wanted to stomp her foot and scream. "Rodney? What are you talking about? I wasn't going anywhere with him. He cornered me in the elevator—against my will."

A flurry of flashes erupted, and questions shouted at them as two paparazzi broke into the lobby.

The elevator doors opened. They escaped, just in time.

Cole led her into his room and sat on the end of the second bed. "Why were you leaving without telling me?"

"After seeing Rodney, I realized I can't do this." Kate's shoulders felt heavy. She didn't want to bare her pain, but she had. "Rosa will soon have a way out for me. Her lawyers have been working on the problem."

"Have they?" Cole massaged his temples and looked at the floor.

****

Realizing Cole wouldn't let Kate go to her room until they had a serious conversation, she moved to a nearby lamb's wool wingback and set her suitcase down. She sank into the chair and sighed. "Why don't you understand, we are doing what is best for you, as her client? Rosa wanted to find what you needed, and she'd concluded you didn't want a soul mate. I was to date you a couple of times, find out what you wanted, and then Rosa would send an appropriate match."

"Very astute of her. Or maybe a cover story for when someone finds out what you two are up to."

"Which would be what?" Kate clapped her hands on her hips, heat burning across her skin.

Hands on hips, he glared at her. "Getting your hooks into unwitting clients' money. Quite a scam. How many other rich men have you snuggled up to?"

Kate froze. This couldn't be happening. Not to someone as kindhearted and honest as Rosa. *How could she fix this?* Against every rule in the universe, she returned her memory to his kiss. Was it to appease the paparazzi, to teach her a lesson, or to prove she was after his money? Either way, the lesson was a valid one. She hated that she'd enjoyed the kiss. "Rosa is the kindest, nicest woman on this planet. She'd do nothing dishonest. And, if you need to ask, then you don't deserve an answer."

Cole's eyebrows arched. "And you? Rodney Hollander III seems to think you aren't being honest."

"Oh, my heavens. One minute I'm running away, and now I'm a selfish gold digger. You can't seem to decide." She jumped to her feet and leaned against the door between their rooms. "I'd be happy to leave, if you'd let me. We can make the paparazzi think we broke up in a way that would suit you. Maybe hint we're still friends."

He shook his head. "No. That won't work for me."

"Why not?"

"I have my reasons, and until I know I can trust you, I don't intend to let you out of my sight. So, for now, you are the person the media believes is my girlfriend. And, for the next couple of weeks, you'll play the role with your heart and soul. That means, we'll have to be comfortable touching each other. You can't flinch every time I touch you." He stood and reached for her hand.

She flinched and slapped his hand away. "That's not fair."

"Why? You entered my life with more bravado than most of my executives do. You've shown you can act."

"It wasn't an act. I'm not afraid of you."

"Aren't you?"

He asked with his sexy, deep voice he used just for her. "No," she squeaked, turning and grabbing for the doorknob.

"If you care nothing about me, why do you panic every time I'm close? I can see it in your muscles. Here, for example." He touched her neck.

His fingers lingered on her skin. His other hand settled on her hip, and Kate's heart thumped inside her chest. Could he feel her fluttering pulse where his hand rested on her neck? Her increased heart rate? Was he measuring her reaction?

"Look at me, Kate." He waited for her response.

"Why?"

"Because I want you to gaze into my eyes and pretend I'm the love of your life. If you can sell it to me, you can sell it to the papers."

"Why do you want me to stay?" She frowned. "I can't pretend something I don't feel. Why not find someone else?"

"Because I've invested time and effort in you. The media think we're a couple. At least, they did until you put your little show on downstairs. Now, they think we have trouble in paradise, and we'll have to re-convince them. I don't have time to find someone else. So, buckle up, baby, you're it."

She frowned. What did he mean? Why didn't he have time? "If I agree to continue with this, I want your guarantee, your promise, not to take Rosa to court, and you won't destroy her business." Kate stared straight into his eyes.

"I promise." He didn't hesitate.

"I want it in writing." She pointed at the pen on his desk.

His mouth twisted. "My word isn't good enough?"

"Not in this lifetime." His laughter startled her.

"You're a breath of fresh air, Ms. Cameron. You keep surprising me. Few people do that."

"Goody." Her throat tightened.

"But what about us? Can you make our

relationship believable for the media?"

She swallowed hard, paused, and considered her words. "I can."

His expression softened.

"Prove it. Right here, right now."

"Honestly? If I think you're going too far for one second, I'll scream it from the rooftops, and that won't be great for your image." She closed her eyes and exhaled.

"I'm just hoping you will be comfortable enough with me to carry this thing off. When we've convinced the world we're a couple and when our contract is up, I'll go away and leave you alone and never bother you again, I promise."

She pressed a hand to her throat. "I'll still need to see on paper that you won't sue Rosa and ruin her business. If you come through with the promise in writing, I will do my best."

"I'll contact my lawyer tonight. The paperwork will be here tomorrow. So, for now, open your eyes, Kate. Make me believe you care about me."

His voice made her panicky. "Okay, I'm looking at you." She gritted her teeth.

"What do you see?" he asked. "Be honest."

Surprised he dared ask, she stopped and considered her answer. "I'm not sure."

"I think you are." He waved a hand down his front. "You see the real me, don't you? The Cole who few people have ever seen."

She frowned. Was he tricking her? She should see the manipulating business executive who forced her to be party to his charade. He had been decent, even though he believed she was part of the scheme against him. Deep down, she considered what would happen if they kissed each other without the constraints of their contract, but that would never happen. "I'm not sure what you mean." She cleared her throat.

"You don't see a billionaire. I think you see the real me. Cole Prentice, bones and blood man, faults and all."

She ran a hand over her eyelids. "Sometimes, I think I see you. Other times, you're just manipulating me." With her hand on the doorknob between their rooms, she eyed him. "Have I passed your test?"

His right eyebrow quirked. "Don't forget the wording in the contract, promising to leave Rosa alone, will be contingent on you keeping up your end of the bargain."

She nodded, then slipped through to her room, slamming the door so hard they'd hear it downstairs. Had she screwed up any chances she'd ever have of escaping the mess she'd put herself in? Worse, she hated her mixed feelings for Cole. One minute he seemed almost human, and the next, she wanted to shove him away and run for home.

Chapter Twelve

Cole dropped onto the side of his bed after hearing the door close. He hated being such a hard-hearted copy of his father. Her trapped expression made his gut clench. He reminded himself he'd caught her and Hollander in the elevator in a more-than-casual embrace. Had she been planning to leave with Hollander on his honeymoon? Of course not. That made little sense, and he'd seen the panic in her eyes. So why had he said such a stupid thing?

His phone rang. "Prentice."

"Cole, what is going on in San Francisco? Weren't you supposed to be improving your image?" Josh sounded frantic.

He straightened the phone, pressing it harder to his ear. "What are you talking about?"

"Just read that you and Kate are fighting in public. Worse, she almost left you high and dry. And then you two argued until you coaxed her back inside the hotel with a very public kiss?"

Flopped back onto the bed, Cole ruffled his fingers through his hair. "Already?" He glimpsed his watch. "It just happened fifteen minutes ago."

"Wow. Because it just broke on the Internet. It'll hit the papers soon."

Not good. Cole heaved a weary sigh. "Josh, do you think Kate Cameron will help improve public relations and save the company?"

"I'm positive. The board is softening. They won't be happy if they find out your relationship with Kate is untrue, though."

Cole closed his eyes. "True, Josh. That's why I'm trying my best to keep Kate on track. As much as she dislikes me, I find her intriguing."

"Again, I'm shocked." Josh chuckled. "You're telling me a pretty face can undo the great Cole Prentice, after all?"

"She's not just a pretty face, and you know it."

"Touchy?"

"I'm not." Punching his pillow, he adjusted his back against the headboard.

"Oh yes, you are." Josh chuckled. "So, how do you intend to salvage the mess you've made?"

"Don't worry, I have a plan."

"Make sure you don't tick her off again. If she doesn't go along, she can ruin this whole thing."

"She won't leave." Cole hated himself for trapping her. She couldn't leave because, black-hearted jerk that he was, he'd made sure of it. Threatening her friend and her own livelihood without blinking an eye meant he'd blackmailed her into staying. The worst part—he'd carry it through if he had to. Josh had been correct, though. The media were more interested in his love life than he'd expected. "We'll ramp up the visibility between us. Prove we're a couple."

"That should help. No more arguments in public, though, okay?" Josh gave a half-hearted laugh.

"I'll try not to. Things seem to get blown out of all proportion between us. I have done nothing to ingratiate myself. She hates me."

"You sure it's hate she's feeling?"

"Yeah, I know dislike when I experience it." Josh's words made his skin go cold. Had he misread Kate's body language?

"Hope you're not losing perspective."

"Me? You know me, Josh. I'm invested in this plan of yours, and I'll make sure we carry it through."

"If anything else goes wrong, make sure you let me know so I can do some damage control before the media gets wind of it the next time."

"Won't happen again. That's a promise." Cole rasped two fingers across his chin. "In fact, I think I have an idea. Book me a high-visibility house on the ocean somewhere on the coast. Make it splashy, with lots of vantage points for the paparazzi to see us. I intend to put on a magnificent show. Lots of candles. Have the fridge well stocked with caviar, champagne—the works."

"I see where you're going with this. You are devious." Josh cleared his throat. "I like it."

"Get back to me with locating a beach-front mansion, asap." Cole vaulted up and paced to the window. "I have a hankering for the ocean. Oh, and be sure to slip and mention to the media where we'll be."

"On it, boss."

Cole gritted his teeth. He'd gone too far to lose the momentum he'd achieved with Kate. She was skittish, and he'd have to make sure she couldn't try to run again. His gut twisted. He hated using her. He had to keep telling himself she had put herself in this position.

Chapter Thirteen

Happy to get out of the hotel and away from Rodney, Kate entered the beach house in Santa Cruz. While she took in the gold-flecked marble tiles, she opened her mouth. Matching gold planters filled with colorful fresh flowers sat on a round table inside the door. Skylights in the stunning vaulted ceiling added just enough light to enhance the layout of the area. She stepped farther inside and spun around. The main area's dimensions were huge. She could put five of her apartments in this spot alone.

When Cole had said they were leaving the hotel for the beach, she assumed they were escaping the paparazzi. Or maybe he just wanted to get her away from Rodney. Didn't matter, she was ecstatic to be out of the hotel and away from her ex. After being propositioned by Rodney, she didn't want to see him ever.

She spun around, getting a full view. The place was a huge three-story modern building with glass windows everywhere. Modern white furniture in perfect placement with glass tables and ultra-soft throw rugs took away from the overwhelming size of the floor space.

The ocean view seemed possible from every direction.

Without waiting for Cole, she stepped outside into

the California warmth and sunshine, enhanced by the fresh scent of a soft ocean breeze. The view was better than she could have imagined. The entire front of the building opened onto a large deck. An infinity pool appeared to spill its turquoise water into the ocean. To the right of the pool sat thick-padded lounges, bright colored umbrellas, and potted plants, creating sections of privacy and shade.

She entered the house again and surveyed the high-end kitchen with every appliance imaginable. "Now, this is only the life a billionaire can have," she whispered under her breath.

"Pardon?" Cole entered the kitchen and set their suitcases down.

"A gal could get used to a place like this." She admired the massive, open-concept kitchen She walked alongside the island, running a hand along the cool, white-and-silver marble, before peeking into the large wine refrigerator—stocked to the brim.

This place gives a whole new meaning to the word pretension. But who wouldn't like it?

Cole let out a long breath and leaned against the island. "At last, a place we can breathe with no one bumping into us at every turn."

She froze. "Is there no one else here? We're all alone?"

"I hope we are alone here."

"I mean, cleaning staff. Housekeeper?"

"No. They rent this place out by the week. The staff comes in and cleans on Sunday, I believe. We'll be alone until then." One eyebrow lifted in a rakish way. "Does it bother you, Kate?"

She bit back a sarcastic retort. "No. I won't have to

pretend to like you here. That suits me just fine."

He grinned.

What the heck was he up to? She frowned.

Dressed in khakis, a T-shirt, and deck shoes—all he needed was a sweater draped over his shoulders to be Ivy League preppy—Cole belonged here.

She bit her lip. "I have to admit, though, I didn't expect to be your prisoner." Irritated they'd be alone, she fought the urge to again run.

"Prisoner? Does this seem like any prison you've ever seen?" He swept his right hand in an outward motion.

"No. But why did we come here? Why didn't we go back to Boston?"

"I told you before, I need a vacation. Since I haven't had one in years, a little fresh sea air would be nice, so here we are."

His dark hair and rugged features sent images of him as a pirate ship captain—eye-patch and all. Maybe the ocean suited him. She bit the inside of her cheek this time.

"What'll we do today?" He gazed around. "Maybe there's a game room with a pool table."

She made an aggravated sound. "If you think I'll keep you entertained, you're mistaken. You stay on your side of the house, and I'll stay on the other."

Hearing him laugh, she clenched her teeth. "I'm not kidding."

"You'd better be kidding. Get your bathing suit on. We'll go for a swim in the pool before dinner."

A quick look toward the massive glass walls showcased the patio and the pool. Heat rippled on the breeze, and a slight ocean breeze rustled her hair through the open patio doors. A dip in the pool would be enjoyable right about now. "No, thanks." She wished she could just get her suit on and jump in, but she didn't want to be easy to control.

He heaved a sigh and stared her down. "Please get your bathing suit on. I expect you to go through the motions, whether or not you like it."

She planted her arms across her chest. "Fine. But I won't enjoy it."

"Fine. Just make it seem like we're happy lovers on vacation."

"What difference would that make? We're alone." A lightbulb flashed in her brain. "We're not alone, though, are we? The paparazzi have followed us. They can see us from almost every room in this…this glass house."

He rolled his eyes. "I hadn't considered that."

"You…you…you manipulator." She slammed her purse onto the couch and raised a hand to slap him.

He held her wrist without exerting pressure.

Rodney would have handled that moment differently.

"Careful."

His loving smile told her everything.

"Long-range lenses might misconstrue your actions. They might think you wanted to slap my face. We can't have that." He wrapped his fingers through hers and yanked her against him.

The full length of his impressive frame flattened against her now. His deep brown eyes laughed into hers.

"Your actions made me do this. Remember that. Besides, I think I'll enjoy proving I'm not as bad as you think."

"Keep your hands off me." Her hands fisted at her sides, ready to push him off.

"Can't."

His voice sounded edgy, while his head lowered.

"Because then it would be impossible to do this…" His mouth touched hers.

His kiss had been light enough she could have withdrawn if she wanted to. But darn it, she didn't want to. Overwhelmed by his spicy scent, and the hard contact with his body spiked her desire meter against her will. When she, at last, gathered some sanity, she pressed one hand against his chest to see if he'd let her go.

He did but tweaked her chin. "You win, this time."

She glanced out the window and hoped the paparazzi enjoyed the show. She sighed. How would she explain this to Rosa? "I'll get my bathing suit."

"Need any help?"

"Not in your wildest dreams." Kate frowned. "Don't get carried away, buster, or I'll be running out the door, contract or not."

"You're the one who agreed to accompany me." He made quotations in the air around the word accompany. "And to help me make believers of the paparazzi."

"Accompany means go out together, to dinner or a function, not anything requiring quotations." She sighed.

One eyebrow quirked. "Well, some of the other ladies who meet billionaires don't feel the same way."

Heat flushed her face. "And I assumed you were being such a gentleman. Now, you've gone and spoiled it all by talking money."

His eyes glittered. "I guess you'd rather be anywhere but here, but I didn't ask to be tricked. This is how you make retribution for your misdeed."

"Why don't you understand our reasons were honorable?" Frantic to escape, she searched for her suitcase and grabbed it.

"Where are you going?"

"To do what you asked. I'll dress in my bathing suit and meet you in the pool." She strolled down a long hallway, looking for a place to change. The bedrooms were huge and decorative. She chose the first one on the left. She returned to the deck.

Cole was already in the pool, doing the breaststroke.

Seeing his powerful arms and lithe body sluicing through the water did little to dispel her anger. In fact, the more she monitored him, the more she resented being forced to act like she cared. Worse, the only bathing suit she'd brought was a yellow bikini. She'd planned to use it, on her own, in the hotel pool.

He'd stopped swimming, treading water in the middle of the pool.

She pretended not to notice the predatory aspect of his gaze. She grabbed a fluffy white towel from a container nearby and spread it out on a lounge.

Cole returned to his laps.

She leaned over, dipping her toes in to gauge the water temperature. She loved swimming, and the cool water enticed her. She took off her bathing suit cover and prepared to jump in when she noticed Cole had stopped swimming.

Treading water, his mouth formed a grim line.

"Why are you wearing that?"

Her spine locked. She wouldn't put her cover back on because of his rude comment. The idiot was making her ashamed of her body, but she had nothing to be ashamed of. She worked out at the gym three days a week, and her toned muscles proved it. "What are you talking about?"

"Get into the water. Hurry."

"Why?"

He swam to her side of the pool and held his hands out. "Jump. Unless you want to be on the cover of every national newspaper in the country with next to nothing on."

"Hey, I have nothing to be ashamed of. This bathing suit covers every..." One flash came from the balcony of the cottage next door, and she dove in headfirst. She stayed under as long as she could hold her breath.

She surfaced.

Cole was waiting.

"How can you live like this?" A little out of breath, she felt sorry for him for the first time.

He paddled away. "You get used to it—sort of."

"C'mon, I've been reading about you in the papers for years. The articles have never been kind. That must have bothered you."

"You've been reading about me? I'm flattered." He swam in circles around her.

No doubt, he believed she was being sarcastic. "Don't be the least bit flattered. I also read about the local criminals and the obituaries." She swam away.

"So, what was it about me that made you want to know more?"

He caught up to her. Geez, he wanted to put on a show for the paparazzi today. "Believe me, you don't want to know."

"Why not?"

She gritted her teeth and turned her back to the veranda hosting the paparazzi. "It's not very flattering."

Another flash. Or was it a light reflecting off a car driving by on the highway? Either way, they both snapped their heads around.

Cole sliced through the water, cradling his arm around her waist. "Don't forget we're putting on a show."

"You have a one-track mind." She grabbed his hand and lifted it over her head, then pirouetted into a dive to the left. After holding her breath underwater, she popped up a distance away.

"Smooth move." His eyes narrowed.

"Sure, the media will love that."

"I'm not positive it's what we need to do to convince them."

Instant goose bumps rose, and she rubbed her arms. *What did he have in mind?* "Is money so important that you'd pimp yourself out?"

He inhaled a sharp breath.

Rather than wait for his angry answer, she swam to the stairs and climbed out of the pool, wrapping herself in a thick towel as fast as possible. She found a lounge chair under an umbrella, in heavy shade, hoping it'd be harder for the paparazzi to get a printable picture.

Cole was still in the pool, but he hadn't taken his gaze off her.

Still acting for his media profile?

"Want a drink?" He floated on his back with his

arms crossed behind his head.

"Have a bartender on the payroll?" She forced a fake grin—she could put on a show, too. Besides, joking from a distance remained safe. But when the separation narrowed, she couldn't afford to get careless.

"No, but I can whip up a few concoctions." He swam to the edge and hoisted himself out. Water dripped off his frame, and he didn't bother toweling off.

Kate swallowed—hard. If his muscles were an indication, he spent plenty of time in the gym. She needed something liquid now, because her mouth had just gone dry. "What are you making?" she asked, for lack of something better to say.

"It's a surprise."

She watched him add juice to the liquor in two glasses but couldn't figure out what he'd made.

"Want to drink it at the bar, or where you are on the lounge?" He followed her gaze. "I see you placed yourself in a strategic position behind a large potted plant. Yeah, that's a good idea." He laughed.

Daring a glance toward the other houses along the beach, she spotted the paparazzi staked out on the deck next door. "Over here, please."

****

Minutes ago, Cole's heartbeat doubled when Kate had removed her bathing suit cover and stood on the edge of the pool in her tiny bikini. Showing off her bod wasn't what he expected. Crazy, but he didn't want to share her with the paparazzi, either. Those buzzards didn't deserve a peek at her toned curves. Grinding his teeth together against losing his resolve, he needed to remember she and Rosa were playing some kind of game. He had to keep things in perspective and play this out to prove himself worthy of being the company's figurehead. If that meant having a fake relationship, he'd manage it, whether or not he liked it.

He pursed his lips and considered how massive this little adventure had become and how it might blow up in his face. He had expected Rosa's match to be more than willing to date a billionaire, so why had she sent someone who disliked him so much and couldn't care less about his riches? Handing Kate a drink, he bent low enough it would seem he was stealing a kiss at the same time.

Kate accepted the glass but cast a wary glance toward the photographers when his face neared hers.

Backing off, he sat in the next lounge.

"I'm curious? How does pretending to have a girlfriend for a couple of weeks improve your image?"

He lifted his glass. *Should he tell her the real reason*? That their time together would be longer than two weeks? Not now, or she'd fly out of here so fast his head would spin. He could tell her part of the truth. "I'm doing this to contain my bad press and to convince the board of directors my position has value."

"Don't you own the company?"

"It's my family's company, but we have investors. If the board wants me out, then my control of the company is gone. I can't allow that to happen. As long as I am CEO, I can secure pension assets." *Darn it. He went too far. Told her too much.*

She frowned at his comment. "I'm confused. Why would your family need investors? You're the richest family in Boston."

He stiffened. He had a limit to what he'd tell her, and discussing his father's inability to run a company, and his father's need to gamble and drink, wasn't something he'd share with anyone. They'd kept it quiet over the years, even after his father contacted the press and said his son had thrown him out—the start of his bad image, forever after perpetuated by the media. He blinked. "How's the drink?"

She glanced at it in her hand. "I haven't tried it yet."

"Taste it."

"I'm not much of a drinker. Two drinks and I'm next to inebriated."

He laughed. "You're kidding."

"Nope."

"In that case, you'll have to go easy on your cocktail because we're having wine with dinner tonight. Can't have you falling over in front of the media." He rolled his eyes and grinned.

"I'm not that bad." She bit her lip. "Are we going out for dinner?"

"No. We're eating in."

She sat forward and narrowed her attention on him. "I might be a mean cupcake maker, but I'm not much of a cook with main dishes."

He could tease her about not being able to cook, but her flushed cheeks and serious expression stopped him. Had it embarrassed her to admit a baker couldn't prepare a meal, so he didn't pursue the topic? He'd cut her a break this time. "Not a problem. I might be a frozen-food king, but I'm also a superb chef. I can whip up some juicy steaks on the barbeque, some baked potatoes and asparagus grilled in garlic butter, and chilled champagne."

"Is this seduction scene for the paparazzi's

benefit?" she asked.

He considered her question. "Not totally. We'll keep the lights low, so they can't see us very well. It'll just be the two of us."

She rolled her eyes. "Sure, whatever."

At first, he lifted a hand toward her, then dropped his arm. "I promise, Kate. For one night, tonight, I'll be the real me. But you must promise to be the real you. No pretenses for one night, okay?" He shifted his position on the lounge, leaned his head back, and stretched his torso.

"Why?" She tipped her head and frowned.

"Because it's tiring. I'm tired of being who you think I am. Aren't you tired of being the woman you're pretending to be?"

Chapter Fourteen

The sun had moved, and the shade was gone. Sunlight warmed her. Kate expected the drink Cole had handed her to be refreshing, but after taking a sip, she made a face at the burn that slid down her throat. It needed more juice—lots more juice. If they had an intimate dinner with no pretenses, she needed her wits, so she set the drink on the small glass-top table.

Number one, she didn't believe he would let his guard down this evening, any more than he believed she would do the same. She glanced in his direction. If his rhythmic breathing was accurate, he'd drifted off to sleep. His drink was on the verge of tipping out of his hand. Maybe he hadn't slept well last night, either.

She doubted he'd spent the night thinking about her. Could she say the same? Had she gone mad? She should be the last person in the world who wanted anything to do with a rich man—or any man. At least for a while. Rodney made sure of that. Fate had been against her this weekend. Either that, or he'd booked into the same hotel to remind her of her mistake?

Slipping the glass from his fingers, she set it down. His hand fell limp. He was sound asleep. Fighting the urge to watch him sleep, she pushed off the lounge and headed inside. Kate needed to call Rosa. At the far end of the dining room, with a view of the patio, she opened her cellphone and found her friend's number.

"Where have you been?" Rosa didn't bother saying hello. "I've been waiting to hear from you."

Kate's heart lifted. She had good news. "Have you found a loophole, Rosa? A way out for me?"

"Oh, hon. I'm so sorry, but no. The lawyers say we can do nothing. But, no matter, I won't ask you to put yourself through this for my company. It's just a business. If I've made a fatal error that takes my business down, then the fault is mine, not yours—come home right away."

Plunking onto one of the plush dining room chairs and pinned her head against the high back of the seat, she stared, unseeing, at the ceiling while her stomach tumbled.

"I mean it, Kate, it's time to come home. I'm so angry that Cole Prentice thinks he can treat you this way."

"No. I'm not coming home. We can't give up yet. I can get us both through this."

"Please, just get out of there. Then I'll tell him where to go!"

Kate lifted her head and scanned the patio area through the open doors. He was still sound asleep—so different and vulnerable. "I think I've talked him into an agreement we can both accept."

Rosa's breath hitched on the other end. "Oh, Kate, I'm so sorry I put you in this position.

"I can't believe I'm saying this, but even with everything that's happened, he's not the horrible person I believed he was."

"What are you saying?" Rosa asked.

Kate imagined the tiny frown lines appearing between Rosa's brows. "Okay, let's consider it this way—he expects me to stay, but I'm not being forced. I could leave right now, and he wouldn't stop me."

"But the threat." Rosa sniffed. "Don't forget about that."

"He has threatened your business if I don't comply, but I think he's a little desperate, and I'm not sure he'd ruin your business."

"Oh no, Kate. Are you falling for another bad boy?"

Kate inhaled. How many other men had offered to cook her such a delicious-sounding dinner? "No, Rosa. I don't know the full scope of what's going on, but I believe he's keeping something from us. He doesn't strike me as the type who'd tear down someone else to save himself."

"But you don't know him, do you? Remember his father? Cole took over the business, leaving his father on the street and penniless. Earl Prentice, his father, did an interview on the television five years ago. The man was a sad mess, let me tell you. And, if Cole Prentice did that to his father, you'd better not get squishy. Don't let him trick you into falling for him."

Kate considered Cole's actions for a second. "Rosa? If he's that bad, why did you take him on as a client?" Rosa had always been an amazing judge of character.

"I don't know. When I met him in person, he seemed serious but genuine. I didn't want to believe all the nasty rumors were true."

"See what I mean. Cole doesn't send out Rodney vibes. He's expecting me to play along and pose as his girlfriend. I must pretend to like him for now, but that's something I can live with. He has tried nothing when we are alone, and he's not ugly by any means." She hoped her dumb joke might make Rosa laugh.

Worst part. Kissing him had not been a hardship, either. In fact, sometimes she found it hard to remember he was forcing her to be here, threatening her business. When his mouth had caressed hers, and he'd held her close…she closed her eyes and took a long breath. She could almost smell his aftershave right now.

Another muffled sob emanated through the phone line before Rosa blew her nose. "It's all such a mess. I've never been so confused and afraid I'd gotten it all wrong. I base my business on reading my clients. Maybe I should just pack it in."

"Don't you dare, and honest, Rosa, it's not that bad." Kate trailed her gaze to Cole again. He wasn't like Rodney. *He couldn't be.* Still, the article showing he'd thrown his father onto the street gave her pause. And, after thinking Rodney was the love of her life, how could she ever trust her ability to judge Cole?

She considered the way Cole had yanked Rodney off her in the elevator. Cole's expression had been murderous, and Kate had to admit she had enjoyed seeing someone put Rodney in his place. She grinned, then chastised herself for being spiteful. She needed to put Rodney's antics behind her and forget about him. In a strange way, Cole had helped her with that. "You know what, Rosa. I think Cole's bark is worse than his bite. At least, I hope so."

"Don't fall for his bad-boy appearance and rugged charm." Rosa made a tsking sound. "I shouldn't have sent you on this mission. Not after Rodney. I'm so sorry to have put you in that position."

Kate laughed. "You haven't realized the best of it

all. Guess who just got married and is staying in the same hotel?"

Rosa paused on the other end. "I dunno…. Who…. Oh! You can't be serious. Rodney was there in the same hotel?"

"And he made a pass at me in the elevator, and Cole caught him and threw him off the elevator onto his derriere."

"This just gets worse and worse." Rosa snickered. "I would have given my eyeteeth to have seen Rodney get his due, though. He deserves more than being tossed onto his rump. Much more."

"It boosted my spirits more than I like to admit. And besides, you know what they say about karma, Rodney will get his payback someday."

"Yeah, right." Rosa laughed louder now. "I wonder if the hotel has CCTV in their hallways. It'd be fun to leak that little video to the press."

"You will not get that footage." Kate slapped her forehead. "Let's just forget the idiot." She sighed. "Back to our problem. I think I've convinced Cole to agree to leave you and your business alone if I go along with this charade."

"Oh, honey, no, I don't like the sound of that."

"Yes, it's okay. He expects me to appear all lovey-dovey in public, but he is civil in private. I can last him out."

Rosa sighed. "I still don't understand why you even had to take those steps to make him promise not to sue me. Honey, this man must know we tried to help him, and it was for the right reasons. If he's really using our good intentions against us, I might have been wrong about him."

"Don't worry. I can handle this situation. I'll be Academy Award worthy for the paparazzi, and they'll believe Cole and I are a couple. Once that is done, I can come home. It'll be game over, and I'll never have to see him again."

"Okay, but if anything changes, if he demands too much—anything at all. My business is not worth your dignity. Do nothing you shouldn't."

Kate ran a hand across her eyes. "If I didn't save your business, I'd be at risk of losing my pride and dignity after all you did for me. Even if you didn't loan me $50,000, you're my best friend. I would have helped you with this, anyway."

"Make sure you remember what I said—there's a limit to what he can ask of you," she whispered. "No matter the consequence."

She sounded worried, as if she didn't trust Kate's judgment on the matter.

"Promise me."

"I promise, Rosa."

"Darn it. I have a client coming in five minutes. I must go." Rosa shuffled papers at the other end of the line. "Call me soon, okay?"

"Will do. This San Francisco gig should be over by the end of the week, then after a few dates the next week at home, our illustrious billionaire will have what he wants, and we'll be free."

They said their goodbyes, and Kate clicked off. She'd forgotten to keep an eye out for Cole. When she lifted her head from putting her cell phone back in her purse, she spotted him leaning against the dining room entrance with his arms crossed over his chest, his eyes glittering.

"Hatching a new little scheme, are we?"

His edgy voice ruffled her already heightened emotions. "No. But if you must eavesdrop on my conversations, you can come to whatever conclusions you wish." Her stomach twisted. She hated that he'd gotten the wrong idea, but by the frown on his face right now, she'd never convince him otherwise. He gripped the side of the door so hard she could see his knuckles whiten.

"You're hard on my head, Kate. One minute I think I have you figured out, and the next minute you prove I was right about you."

She stood.

His expression changed to instant predator.

One look, a potent reminder she was still in her bikini. Any fool could see he liked her body. The truth hit hard. As much as she feared he'd end up being another callous rich man who wanted her for what she could do for him, she didn't believe it, not deep down.

"Can you cover yourself up?" His teeth had clenched.

Instant mortification burned through her and heated her cheeks. She pursed her lips and marched past him, her head high. She could feel her breasts bouncing in her skimpy bikini top but could do nothing about it now.

"I'll cook dinner in an hour," he shouted.

Ignoring him, she strode down the hallway toward the bedroom she'd picked. She had a hot shower, washed her hair, then dressed in a wrinkle-free light-green sundress. She'd play his game until her two weeks were up, even if it killed her. He was planning a fancy dinner and show for the paparazzi tonight, so she'd go along and play the part.

The dress she chose enhanced her shape. The low neckline showed a hint of breast, with a flowing floral skirt slit up one side to mid-thigh. A cool, semi-casual dress for a tropical location. She'd wear matching green high heels and would stand almost eye to eye with Cole. But first, she'd lean back on the puffy pillows until time for dinner.

His distant voice jerked her awake.

She jumped up, ran a brush through her hair, adjusted her lipstick, and met him in the kitchen. She should have offered to help him cook, but she needed to stay away as much as possible.

Dusk had fallen, and at least a dozen lit candles flickered on the deck. The patio appeared to be a typical seduction scene. Despite her overwhelming fear, she couldn't help but feel satisfied she had dressed the part. He couldn't tell Rosa that she hadn't kept up her part of the bargain. She made her way to the balcony.

Cole stood at the barbeque dressed in khaki pants and a white polo shirt.

He knew how to dress to enhance his tan and broad shoulders. "You've been busy." The balloon of disquiet grew in her stomach.

"Barbequing is easy."

He waited, as if he sensed something was off in her voice. His features were softer than they had been when she'd flounced off in her bikini.

"Did you have a nap?"

"Yeah. Sorry, I didn't help with dinner. I just meant to close my eyes for a minute."

"Not a problem. You needed the rest. Besides, if we do this thing right, we can go home and meet for dinner once a week."

He'd spoken in such a low voice, she strained to hear him. "That would be acceptable."

"After seeing you like this tonight, not a sane man in the world would believe I'd be with a beautiful woman like you and not have ulterior motives."

"Except you have ulterior motives." Kate pressed her hands together. "Just not any you want them to know about."

His eyes shuttered. "I guess we've both done things we can't undo. Not if we want our businesses to succeed."

She closed her eyes while her hopes and dreams teetered on the brink. If this failed, she could lose her business, too, especially if the paparazzi searched her history and found the vile articles from the past. She bit the inside of her cheek.

Cole approached her. "Tonight, we let our guard down and be ourselves. Forget about the media over there. Let's celebrate." His voice carried across the patio.

"I'm just glowing with excitement." Her words came through gritted teeth. She hadn't forgotten their audience on the next patio over. Of course, everything he'd just said was for them, not for her. He touched her hair, and her nerve endings caught fire at the mere brush of her bare shoulder, she shivered. She faked a laugh, wondering if she appeared nervous. "Sounds like heaven." She spoke loud enough to be heard on any listening devices down the beach.

He winked. "I believe I could make you say those words and mean it."

This time, he'd spoken just to her. She could

almost believe what he'd said. Almost—then she wrenched herself back to reality. His actions were always an act for the paparazzi. If he manipulated her as much as he did the media, then she couldn't trust him. She blew out a breath. "And just how far do you expect me to go to save my company?"

He swept her into his arms and placed one finger over her lips. "Darling, you love to tease. Are we playing games tonight? Did you pack your Swedish Maid outfit?"

She frowned.

He ignored her expression and bent to nibble her earlobe. "They have a listening device tonight, if I'm not mistaken."

"Wait. Is that legal?"

"Hell if I know. All I know is we'll have to be very careful about what we say to each other."

His warm breath on her neck, and his voice whispering in her ear sent goose bumps flaring across her bare flesh. "You always know how to drive me to the brink of ecstasy." She mouthed in a robotic monotone.

He cocked his head. "Hey, stop playing with me."

His arms wrapped around her. What did he plan to do next? Knowing she could do better, she tipped her head back and smiled up into his eyes. "You know how I feel about you, my darling. You are my moon and stars." She put more emotion into it this time.

He rolled his eyes, because his back was to the paparazzi. His expression lightened, and he grinned. "And I intend to keep it that way, my love. It's been love at first sight for me. You make my heart sing."

While he sounded convincing enough, his gorgeous

brown eyes appeared disinterested. Almost as if he didn't believe she could do this thing as well as he did. His lack of belief in her was like a red flag. Gauntlet dropped. He wasn't the only one who could act. She ran an index finger along his bottom lip. "I wonder, do you taste as delicious as you appear tonight?" She leaned in to give him an ever-so-slow kiss along the edge of his mouth.

He met her mouth and turned the kiss into a bone-searing, full-on make-out session. By the time he'd stopped, she was gasping.

Drawn closer in his arms, she noted his predatory expression. She brushed her fingers against his ear in an intimate gesture.

"And she can act," he whispered. "Be careful, my darling. You might even make me believe."

Her hands were flat on his chest. She hoped he would let her go if she applied any force, and maybe that's why she allowed this. She had to think of this as a three-act play. Should she stretch her arms up around his neck or brush him off? How far would she go for this charade? What was her next big idea?

He cupped her shoulders, then turned toward the ocean. "It's a beautiful night, my love. A perfect night for the two of us to be here alone."

Gag. He'd gone overboard. She hated he could make her heart race whenever he hinted at intimacy. "But first, we need sustenance, sweetie. We haven't eaten since breakfast, and that sizzling steak smells great."

He leaned down and kissed her.

Lighter this time…a tease. Payback for the kiss she'd just given.

"Maybe I enjoy being an actor," he whispered.

"You're very sure of yourself," she returned.

His laugh carried on the breeze.

She recognized his genuine laugh. He seemed to like it when she put him in his place.

Picking up a remote, he tuned into relaxing orchestra music. "It should be a little harder for them to hear us now. But we still must be careful."

He pressed a gentle index finger against her lips.

She leaned away from his touch because it set off dangerous sensations she needed to ignore.

"Here's hoping this performance will assuage the media and prove to my board I'm the figurehead they want."

Noting the concern in his voice, against all sanity, she wanted to make things better.

But he let her go and strode to the grill to attend to his barbequing.

Kate thought about his statement. She'd bet he'd just given away more information than he wanted to. Maybe because he was being forced into this, too. She couldn't blame him for wanting to keep the reins of his family's business. If he had been upfront with her, then she would have been more compassionate. She'd experienced the heartache of fighting for her business. She reminded herself to keep her own cupcake enterprise in mind during the evening's ordeal, because everything was at stake.

"Dinner's ready."

He'd set the table with proper glasses and silverware. "You did a fantastic job setting the table. Where'd you learn how to do that?

"I worked as a server in my university years."

"Uh-huh." Did she believe him? Why would a rich family expect their son to work at university? Because he needed to learn responsibility? Maybe.

He had set ocean-themed dishes, complete with silver cutlery and fresh-cut roses, in a vase in the center of the massive table. Wine glasses, cloth napkins, and cutlery laid in all the right places. "You sure we're alone? Someone else didn't set the table?"

"Positive." He grinned.

The smell of grilled steak wafted on the breeze, along with sizzling onions and mushrooms. California red wine breathed on the table. She approached the grill and peered at the steak for a second before she strayed her gaze to Cole.

"Do you like what you see?" he asked.

She tore her gaze from him. "Sorry?"

"The steak. Is it done enough?"

Good thing he hadn't picked up on what she'd been thinking, and it wasn't beef. "Oh right. I like it medium-well." She inhaled the delicious odor.

He smiled. "Perfect. It's done then." He took the steaks off the grill, put them on a platter, and leaned close. "Have a seat, and remember, no frowns or indications that you can't stand me, okay?"

"Okay." She hesitated. Is that what he believed? That she couldn't stand him? Of course, he'd given her every reason to feel that way, so why didn't she? Maybe that's what he believed. Couldn't blame him, either, if he assumed she and Rosa were scamming him. *What a mess!*

Picking up the remote, he changed the music to easy listening.

Perfect for their meal. It added to the overall

ambiance, with the beach in clear view. The tide ebbed, and waves swished over the sand, while the moon hung heavy in a sky full of stars. She inhaled. "I love ocean air."

"Me, too." He set the platter down in the center of the table. "But right now, I love the smell of steak more. Don't know about you, darling, but I'm starving."

Did he need to use such an adoration? Could the paparazzi hear them over the music?

He held out her chair, and for just a second, his fingers brushed the back of her neck.

Had it been deliberate? She shivered.

He returned to his side of the oblong glass patio table, and he poured two glasses, then produced a platter of steaming baked potatoes and asparagus from the top part of the barbeque grill. He sat opposite her and raised his glass. "To you, Kate. May your dreams come true."

A crazy, fat tear threatened. If he had any idea how he had dashed her dreams, he'd never have toasted her. "To success and getting everything you deserve—in business." She didn't force it.

He winked. "If you don't dig in, then I'll start without you." He picked up his fork.

She heard his stomach rumbling. She laughed, then picked up her knife and fork and cut a square of her tender beef. It melted in her mouth. "Delicious."

His smile lit up at her compliment. He made comfortable small talk throughout dinner, and they took their time finishing the bottle of wine over an amazing dessert made from canned peaches, ice cream, bourbon, and whipped cream.

"This dessert tastes like you slaved over it all day." She wiped the edges of her mouth with the napkin.

He laughed. "Yeah, I learned to impress the girls with this recipe at university. Since I worked part-time in a restaurant, a guy can pick up some cooking ideas. Helps to know how to do that when the budget is tight."

She frowned. "You don't expect me to believe you had to work your way through university?" She lowered her tone, so the paparazzi couldn't hear.

He picked up his napkin, wiped his mouth, then threw it on the table. He leaned back, satisfied. "Yep. I did." He raised the volume with the remote so they could talk without being overheard.

"Did your family want to teach you responsibility?"

"No. I had to earn my way through university. Having money on paper doesn't always mean free-flowing cash in hand. I'm sure, as a businesswoman, you understand."

She leaned forward. "Yes, I do, but I'm confused. I understand the logistics of business, but you come from one of the richest families in Boston."

"Even affluent people experience difficulties when markets take a downturn." His gaze shifted toward the paparazzi. "Let's change the subject, shall we?"

Of course, she'd always expected he'd had nothing but a life of abundance, with no worries about having to scrounge for work, or education. She'd been wrong, and she'd bet more than the economy caused his troubles.

A furtive glance toward the several men and women hanging over the patio railings of the beach house next door showed cameras on tripods pointed in their direction. She lowered her voice. "Why are they allowed to invade our privacy?"

"Freedom of the press, I guess. I've never considered the legalities of their pursuits. But then, until you arrived, the women I dated were happy to go along with the propaganda machine. I guess they enjoyed seeing themselves in the news." He grinned while reaching over and interlocking his fingers with hers. He lifted her hand and kissed it. "And with this dress on, there's no doubt you'll elevate both of us to the society pages tomorrow."

"Why? What do you mean by my dress?" She ran a hand over the soft folds.

"You're beautiful. That's all I'm saying."

"Oh! Thank you." For once, she swallowed an instant retort but wondered how much of what he'd said was honest?

A gust swirled off the ocean and blew out several of the candles. Cole raised his right arm and clicked the remote to another type of music. A waltz. "Care to dance?"

She wanted to say *no*, but of course, this was all part of the show, and she'd promised to do her very best. "I can't wait." She laid her napkin on the table and stood.

His expertly created lustful expression washed over her. "I promise not to step on your toes."

"I'm sure you've had lots of practice." She wished all this faux bantering would stop. If he dared kiss her again, then she'd combust.

He held out a hand, then swung her into his arms, and they swayed to the music as if they'd always danced together, almost floating on air.

"Did you plan this?" she asked, her mouth close to his ear.

"What?"

"Changing the music so we could waltz?"

He tipped his head back and smiled. "And if I did?"

She sighed. "Nothing. It's nice. I haven't waltzed in a very long time."

He spun her around.

She caught sight of a few flashes going off.

"We dance well together. Like we've danced together for years."

"Hmmm. Think that'll sell papers?"

"Let's forget about them. We're being real, remember? Ourselves."

"It's not so easy to act believable, given the circumstances. Being under the scrutiny of the papers and all, but I'll try my best." She faked a smile in his direction. Not nearly as soul-shaking as the look he'd just given her.

"Thanks. I appreciate it."

This kinder, gentler version of Cole Prentice made her a little nervous. She wanted him to stay edgy. That way, she'd have a fair idea about where she stood and how to hold her own against him. Like this, dancing the night away she was in danger of forgetting Cole Prentice's true agenda. "If we're being real tonight, Cole, how does being in a set-up location, with a set-up meal, and a set-up date under a backdrop of stars, next to a soothing surf in California, make it feel real to a girl from Boston?"

He laughed low in his throat. "Good point. But this is as real as we can get right now." He rested his chin against the side of her hair. "Either way, I'm enjoying dancing with you, and who knows, maybe if we'd met under different circumstances, this would've been possible without faking it."

Kate stiffened.

But he didn't let her go. "Relax. It's just the wine talking."

She had to admit he'd been making her more comfortable by creating a façade of believability when he tipped her chin up and forced her to smile.

"Close your eyes, listen to the music, and the waves." He spun her around the deck again. "Don't think about anything else—that's my plan."

She leaned her head against his shoulder and closed her eyes. All she could think about was this oversized male's body so close. His clean scent and powerful arms, his lips so close to her hair. The sensual tempo and movement of their bodies to the music created a heady moment. Tantalizing and tempting— too easy to let emotion sway her.

While they continued waltzing, she allowed herself to fall deeper under this rhythmic spell. Somehow, she relaxed. Her lack of tension sent the wrong message, because his head lowered, and his mouth captured hers. Blinding lights snapped her back to reality.

She should have been more aware of the paparazzi, but at this moment—she didn't care. She squeezed her eyes shut. While forcing herself back to reality, she reminded herself never be a pawn again. It scared her she'd come dangerously close tonight. No way could she lose perspective over a single kiss. He was manipulating her. She needed to remember that. And, at the touch of his kiss, she kept it light and tantalizing.

They continued dancing, waltzing, living in the moment until—she realized the music had stopped. "Cole?"

"Umhummm?"

"The music isn't playing any longer."

"Ahhh, but I still hear the melody. The ocean is playing just for us." His lips pressed against her ear.

Ignoring the heat of his body against hers, she focused on the swish of the waves caressing the sandy beach, mixed in with the sounds of the breeze playing through the plants and wind chimes on the patio. They were moving to the music of nature itself. His body heated hers while the cool breeze of the ocean drafted over them.

No matter how fake the scenario, she admitted the evening was enjoyable. Too enjoyable. If his chin tipped even the slightest, could she ignore his kiss this time? She wanted to kiss him again. Her willpower had dwindled to near nothing in the last few minutes. In desperation to get hold of herself, she jerked away.

He froze for a second, then let her go. Mouth in a thin line, he led her to a grouping of padded chairs under potted palm trees dotted with tiny LED lights.

A fresh bottle of wine sat in ice on the table.

When had he put it there? She raised a brow. "More wine?"

"Champagne this time."

As if they were alone in a little magical realm. The deck had gone dark except where twinkling mini lights dotted the leaves of two potted palm trees.

Hearing him clear his throat, she stepped toward a single chair.

"Not there, Kate. Sit beside me on the loveseat."

She'd rather not, but his comment made sense. She was here to do a job and didn't want to disappoint Rosa. Maybe Cole would soften if Rosa found his genuine match. Waltzing, and then snuggling with Cole Prentice, was the last thing she wanted. She could tell herself that.

The flashes of camera light proved the paparazzi lapped their interaction up.

She sat with his arm wrapped around her shoulders. "Let's not get carried away, Prentice." She stiffened in his grasp. She could only manage so much touchy-feely tonight. She'd hit her limit.

Removing his arm, he leaned forward to pour each of them a glass of wine. "Things are going well. Aren't you enjoying yourself?" he asked in a low, serious voice.

"Do you think they can hear us?" she asked.

"I hope not, but you never know."

That explained a few of his comments. She should have known he didn't mean the things he'd said, but somewhere deep down she'd wanted his words to be honest. How sad was that? Was she so desperate?

Tidying her hair, she took a fortifying breath. *No.* A rich man was not in her cards—never again. If she fell for his act, she'd end up in shreds. She had to wake up; otherwise, she'd have learned nothing from her fiasco with Rodney Hollander III.

Chapter Fifteen

Cole sighed. Playacting on the balcony stretched his limits, because he'd been thinking about Kate way too often. He needed to remember she'd tried to manipulate him. But when he smelled the floral scent of her shampoo, he forgot everything. Something about her, right down to her scent, broke through his wall of defense. She could not be his match—ever. This was all for show.

When he handed her a glass of champagne, he saw she didn't look happy—his own fault she didn't trust him. Why should she? He'd forced her to come here, threatened her business, and that of her friend. She was an unwilling participant in this pretense. Yet, every time he'd kissed her, to keep up appearances, the barrier he'd built against her slipped.

He had to remain impartial and to remind himself he was the worst kind of beast. He forced her to do this against her will. How could he ever expect her to forgive him? How could he forgive himself?

Taking the first step gave both her and Rosa full release from any wrongdoing or threat of a lawsuit, even though Kate didn't know yet. He had had the document drawn up this morning. Kate would get it when she arrived home, and Rosa would receive the document at the same time.

He glanced at Kate again. His chest felt tight. He

could lose himself in her. She drove his feelings into unchartered waters. With the sexy dress she wore tonight, he was having a hard time not touching. And continuing the charade had become difficult—to pretend she didn't mean something to him.

They had chemistry that could go nuclear if he wasn't careful. He wanted to make love to her. But he wanted it to be in an atmosphere of mutual trust and respect. Not under the umbrella of threat and fear of being on the cover of tomorrow's newspaper.

Even he wasn't that big of an idiot. Was he?

Chapter Sixteen

After an interminable time, Kate stifled a yawn, then checked her watch before whispering in his ear, "Have we given the paparazzi enough of a show tonight? I'm getting tired." Truth was, she couldn't take much more pretense. She was about to throw herself at him. If he gave her one more of those burning hot, I-want-your-body gazes, then she might give in. She was pretty sure the cameras couldn't capture his lustful gazes from the balcony next door.

Before she could lean away, she felt his fingers on the strap of her dress. She froze. If he let her strap slip down her arm, what would she do? Run, or stay, and enjoy the moment?

It surprised her when he straightened her strap again and slid a body's length away from her.

"You didn't drink your champagne."

He sounded reluctant to call it a night, but he'd physically put distance between them. "No, I had enough earlier." Not that she would tell him, but she needed to remain composed when she was near him.

Open to public view, see-through patio glass wrapped around the balcony—a visual reminder of the optical nature of their faux-relationship. She spotted the glowing embers of several cigarettes on the deck on the next balcony. "I feel sorry for actors. How can they stand being under a magnifying glass all the time?"

Cole shrugged. He leaned over to hike up the music on the speaker behind her. "I know I don't like it. But somehow, I fell into the slot of being the bad-boy, media-making-member of my family. Because the media's perception about my personal life has elevated the company's exposure, it makes me newsworthy. And, good or bad, being newsworthy makes money for the company. It has affected my plans to win over the board, however. They think I'm reckless and a terrible choice for CEO of the company."

Again, his truth surprised her. "But don't you own the majority share? They can't oust you, can they?"

His expression became taut, and he gave a non-committal shrug while glancing toward the paparazzi.

The air hung mute between them until Kate spoke. "Do you think they'll follow me around when we get home?"

He tipped his head. "That's a given. Maybe it'll give your cupcake business a boost?"

"I'm thinking that kind of coverage is something I don't need. No offense."

"I don't think it'll damage your business. In fact, it could give you a little more visibility if you market it right."

She lifted an eyebrow. *If he didn't sue her.*

He laughed. "No, I'm not coercing you into anything."

She shrugged.

He set his glass down. "I've decided since the paparazzi are not giving up, we might as well go home tomorrow. They can spy on us there just as well. Besides, I have some work to do when we get back."

Had this pretense been as difficult for him as for

her? She realized he appeared tired.

Going home forced her into creating a grand finale for the media. Freedom loomed sweet and lustrous. A little more acting, and she could tie this thing up.

She could do it. But how would Cole take it? Her heart ratcheted up. She was going for it. In one motion, she slid closer. Feeling like a total fake, she ran her hand up one of his sinuous arms, then wrapped her fingers into the neatly trimmed, soft hair at his nape.

Camera flashes were blinding.

His gaze met hers, molten. "Kate, you're convincing me, too," he whispered.

She laughed. A tinkling, false tone she hoped sounded genuine enough to people who didn't know her. She stood and hauled him to standing. Her hand in his, she led him across the patio. She'd upped the ante and flipped one strap off her dress just before they entered the house.

The thought occured that she might've gone overboard with the tease when Cole's interest didn't lessen in the hallway's privacy. In fact, he was still holding her hand. She let go and expelled a breath. "This stuff is exhausting."

"You give new meaning to *still waters run deep.* Deep, beautiful, and as sensual as any woman I've ever met."

She flushed. She hadn't expected him to say anything like that. "Wait, don't forget, you consider me a scammer."

He nodded and allowed a slow grin, then took two steps closer. "Scam me all you want, lady. I'm sold."

"You must be an easy sell. I'm not that good at acting. I just wanted to wrap this thing up and make our…relationship…appear indisputable so we can go home tomorrow." She sighed.

"You're saying you had an ulterior motive, but what about being ourselves tonight?"

"Sure. We were real, weren't we?"

He slipped an arm around her waist.

She stiffened when his fingers settled against the small of her back, nudging her closer.

"The outside walls are glass, but the inner rooms are solid. We are alone now."

"I noticed." She inched back. "And I'm glad, aren't you? I'm sure you're not an exhibitionist, any more than I am." She laughed, but it sounded weak.

"We could have even more privacy. It's as easy as this." He held up the universal remote to close the patio doors, then the clear glass shifted to charcoal.

"Hey, cool. How does it work?"

"Not sure." He grinned. "I'm just glad it does." He continued to hold her tight.

The heat built between them. She was both terrified and tempted. She inched her fingers up his arms to touch his shoulders. "Maybe we're getting carried away with this playacting?" With that, she gave him a playful shove to put distance between them, reminding herself he wasn't her actual date. He was the man forcing her to be here.

He rubbed the back of his neck. "Maybe we *should* get carried away and get the sensual tension out of our system."

"That would be a bad idea," she whispered, feeling heat behind her eyes. No way would she cry and show Cole how upsetting his kiss had been, as if he cared, rather than his $40,000 investment.

"How bad?"

His voice grated over her, turning her words into innuendo. "Although I'm sure you're used to women falling at your feet, you must know by now I'll never be your pawn, even if we are softening a little toward each other."

"Ah, we're playing chess now, are we? Let's see." He leaned closer, then glanced at her earlobe.

Heat flushed her skin, reminding her of when he'd kissed her there, and he noticed. Darn him.

He smiled. "Checkmate?"

How easy was she? This was a man she wanted to detest, but right now, all she could think about was what a great kisser he was. Worse, from the moment she'd met him, an inexplicable electricity arced between them, which made her think she must need her head examined. This man might not be dangerous, but he *was* dangerous. Any attraction made little sense. And yet, she hated to admit she was. What would Rosa think about the sad truth? Kate had allowed herself to fall for the frozen food king?

He watched her. "I think you want this as much as I do."

She tipped her head up and kissed him without regretting it for the first time. No one was watching. This wasn't for show. She had to make sure her willpower didn't spiral out-of-control right now. She pulled back. "Maybe we're too good at playacting." She put some distance between them. "Because I think we're getting carried away with the moment, and we're beginning to believe our manufactured fairy tale." She flattened her hands against her hot cheeks. "To be honest, I didn't expect to get carried away, not with another rich man." Her breath hitched.

"You're right. I'm sorry, I shouldn't have…"

"Wait. A rich man?" He frowned. "You can't tar every man who has money with the same brush as Rodney. He's not the example to measure men by."

"Let's just forget it, okay? You and I are in a strange situation. We don't like each other much, even though we seem to have serious chemistry. I think the whole seduction scenario tonight has gotten way out of control."

He nodded but still regarded her with raised eyebrows.

"I'm sorry. I didn't mean to insult you." She paused. "It's not you…"

"It's me…" He laughed. "Listen, forget about it. I'm sure the paparazzi bought our act, and I thank you. You've done what I'd hoped you'd do. Even if you say you don't care about the size of my wallet, it's beside the point."

"Believe it or not." Had he said that on purpose? To make her angry? It worked, because it irritated her plenty. Rodney might have left her in financial trouble, but she'd seen the same self-serving, uncaring traits in some of his friends. Her experience had left her jaded. Only someone special could change her mind, but so far, Cole hadn't proved to be any different. Which made her attraction even harder to explain.

Cole didn't know she was an orphan, with no idea who her biological parents were. Words Rodney had used against her when she asked him to help her with the venue payment. Driving her fingernails into her palms, she prayed for a moment of sanity, because she still wanted to wrap her arms around Cole's neck and crush her breasts against him until her mouth captured his.

"Believe it or not, Kate, this entire experience is new to me, too. Our convoluted feelings are hard to explain." He ran a hand across the back of his neck. "It would be a lot easier if you were a gold digger."

Her heart swelled, and she instantly wanted to hug him but thought better of it. He didn't believe she was out for whatever she could get. "I suggest we avoid night time dinners and dancing on the patio."

"Maybe a good idea. We've done enough acting for them. If they won't swallow what happened here tonight, nothing will make them believe we're a couple. One good thing might have come out of this, though. We've created a kind of truce between us, haven't we? We can tolerate each other, at least."

She nodded, still tongue tied by his admission, and she decided to put distance between them. Over the past week, they'd both said things that were less than charitable about each other. *How had he decided she wasn't a gold digger?* All the playacting had been taxing. Right now, she just wanted to get some sleep, then go home, and back to normal life. "Which room are you sleeping in?" She glanced down the hall at the four bedroom doors.

One eyebrow lifted.

Had he expected her to change her mind? "No, that's not what I meant. What if the paparazzi are in a boat with a long-range lens? These windows are floor to ceiling." She dramatized a shiver.

"I can darken the windows. But the bedrooms have heavy curtains hidden inside wall pockets. When I tried the remote control in my room I found them by mistake." He winked.

"Perfect. Before you go to bed, would you use the remote to close the curtains in my room?"

"Sure. Do you know where the remote is?"

"I think I saw it on the bedside table."

He entered her room. "Right. There it is." With the touch of a couple of buttons, he closed her curtains. "I agree. It's a good idea to have me shut your curtains. If the paparazzi are on the ocean, they'll see the two of us together. I'll keep my lights out when I go to bed, so they won't know we're in two separate rooms." He paused, then handed her the remote. "It works for the TV, too, if you can't sleep." He stepped into the hall and looked back. "Good night."

"Good night." Eyeing the king-sized comfy bed, she closed the bedroom door and crawled into her pajamas. She couldn't wait to sink in and sleep. The evening had been harder on her emotions than she'd expected.

Early the next morning, she awoke in a cloud of comfort. The mattress was the most amazing thing she'd ever experienced. The thought of going through the motions with Cole again today made the feeling of happy lethargy drain from her. He'd said they could tolerate each other, but did it mean he'd forgotten any threat to her business?

At least, they were going home today. That was one blessing. As soon as her feet touched the soil of home, she'd get as far away from Cole Prentice as possible. Sudden tears burned behind her eyelids, but she blinked them back. No way would she give in to feeling sorry for herself. She'd gotten herself into this situation. Rosa hadn't forced her to take on the job.

She showered and dressed in a pair of lime-green capris and a matching short-sleeved blouse, then made her way into the main part of the house. The rich aroma of coffee greeted her halfway down the hall, luring her into the kitchen. Cole had been cooking again. She smelled bacon. The stove and counters were empty, but she found scrambled eggs and a fluffy stack of homemade waffles in the warming oven. He wasn't kidding when he said he could cook. She'd never in her life made waffles, and these were homemade.

With no sign of Cole in this part of the house, she helped herself to bacon, waffles, and scrambled eggs from a warming tray. After washing her dishes, she took her coffee to the patio in search of Cole.

He was in the pool, stroking through the water.

Standing near the edge of the pool, she sipped hot, rich coffee and waited for him to notice her.

He stopped swimming and smiled. "Morning. Did you find breakfast?"

She nodded. "I hope you didn't want me to wait? I already ate and enjoyed every bite." His smile made her heart skip a beat.

Treading water, he nodded. "I'm an early riser. I ate quite a while ago."

"And you made breakfast for me, too. You didn't have to." She took a sip of her coffee.

He laughed. "It's easy." He swam to the side and climbed out of the glistening turquoise water. Sunlight glinted off the droplets on his chest.

She tugged sunglasses out of her pocket, then put them on. Maybe he'd have a harder time reading her emotions if she hid her eyes. Or that she couldn't tear her gaze away from his impressive body right now.

And, look at the two of them—having a normal conversation.

His sexy smile threatened to turn her knees to malleable putty if she didn't get a grip on herself. She swept a glance to the deck next door, half hoping the paparazzi would be there, and giving them a reason to kiss. They were gone. By Cole's reaction, she guessed he was aware.

The blinders were tearing off like a painful bandage, reminding her the whole thing had been an act. Nothing more. She moved to a deck chair in order to lounge in the sun.

He threw on a T-shirt, then pointed at her coffee cup. "Join me for a refill?"

"Sure." She rose.

But he waved her back down. "Stay. I'll bring the carafe out here, because it's too nice to sit inside."

"Can you carry everything yourself?" she asked.

He winked. "I'll use a tray. You might think I'm a spoiled rich boy, but I can take care of myself. I have skills that would surprise you."

Oh, she'd noticed his skills, all right. As good as they were, she didn't want a reminder.

They were silent when they drank their coffee. The ocean hissed over the sand, and Kate closed her eyes. She wanted to remember the sounds and scents of California. So different from home.

He drained his cup, then set it on the tray.

"What time are we leaving?" she asked, peering over the last sip.

He picked up the carafe. "Whenever you're ready."

"Doesn't the plane leave at a certain time?"

"Not when it's my plane. I'll just tell the pilot to

file a flight plan. It'll be done by the time we pack up to leave for the airport. I already filed a general flight plan for today, anyway."

Silence hung between them like dead air. The pretense was over, and she already sensed a difference in his attitude toward her. She rose and leaned against the railing overlooking the ocean. Too bad she hadn't had the chance to dip her toes in the ocean before they left, but she had no intention of spending any more time here than necessary. "Well, I suppose I should go pack my luggage."

He put the carafe and cups back on the tray and set it on the patio table. "I think we need to talk first."

Her heart stuttered. He sounded so serious. "Yes?"

"Kate, you and I have chemistry. I think we found out last night."

A knot formed in her chest, but no words would come out.

"In fact, we have killer chemistry." He made eye contact.

Her chest tightened. "You already said that."

"I'd like to make a proposition." He ran a hand over his chin but still didn't look straight at her.

She bit her lip before speaking.

"Another one?" Her stomach erupted with butterflies, but not the good kind. What was he up to? Besides, wasn't it his fault she'd nearly let her guard down last night? She was thankful things hadn't gone too far. But he had tempted her. What was wrong with her?

"It's about us."

She didn't miss how his tone slipped over her like silk. He sounded casual, but his body language said otherwise. Her heart skipped several beats. "What about us?"

"I'm sorry," he began. "Last night, I shouldn't have…"

"If this is about the kiss in the hall, I agree it shouldn't have happened," she cut in. "I understand your regret this morning. Let's just chalk it up as a mistake and forget about it, shall we? Like you said, we can tolerate each other if we must."

He frowned while glancing at the ocean.

Kate shifted her arms over her chest and bit her lip. "I'm not sure I like where this is going."

"I don't regret the kiss, Kate. Not for one second."

The flush burned up her neck now. "It shouldn't have happened." She looked away.

"I want you to stay with me."

His gaze melted into her. "What do you think I am doing right now?" She half-laughed, maybe out of nervousness, because he seemed so serious right now.

"No. When we get home, too." He paid serious attention to the tiles on the deck. "Longer than the requested two weeks."

All the muscles in her lower back tightened—she couldn't budge. "You must be joking. You promised if I carried through with this trip, the blackmail would be over."

Cole's mouth pinched. "I wouldn't call it blackmail."

"What would you call it, then?"

"Mutual negotiations. I used the same tactics you and Rosa used—only you weren't honest with me."

"And threatening my business and Rosa's?" She didn't hide the building anger in her voice.

"That was wrong, and I admit it. I've received the legal documentation proving I won't carry out those threats. My lawyer faxed the papers this morning."

She raised an eyebrow and searched for a fax machine.

"You don't rent a place like this without all the amenities. I made sure I'd have an office. It's at the back of the house." He took a folded sheet out of his shirt pocket and extended it.

She scanned the sheet. It appeared legitimate. "Thanks for this." Her heart squeezed. She had no intention of continuing their façade when they got home. She needed to get back to a quiet, normal life. "I'll have to talk to Rosa before I comment further."

"I'm sorry things happened the way they did."

Another remark she hadn't expected. She regretted last night, in part because her feelings had changed—against her better judgement.

"Your answer?"

"To what?"

"To continuing our relationship for the benefit of our media profile?"

Lightbulb moment. For the media. "Nope. I'm surprised you'd suggest it. You've been very clear. You believe I tried to scam you? Now that Rosa knows what you want in a relationship, I'm sure she can find the right woman for you. A woman of means who can fit into your world."

He frowned. "The media believes we're a couple…"

She raised a hand. "Don't. I have a limit to where I'll go and what I'll do." She swallowed hard. Crying right now would be easy, not that she'd let him know how she felt. She could understand why he'd think she'd be easy, given the way she'd kissed him last night. "For your information, I'm done being your pretend girlfriend. Since I carried out my end of the bargain, I just want to go home—to my home." *And forget last night.* Her nerves became brittle, as if she could break apart at any moment.

Even though they had a chasm of irreconcilable differences, Cole had, in part, redeemed her feelings toward him. For instance, she'd seen him in a different light after he'd taken her side and made Rodney back down in the elevator. He'd said she wasn't an opportunist.

She blinked back a tear. She was being a romantic fool. He was a billionaire who'd forced her to play by his rules, and for a moment, she'd let herself believe her feelings could be real.

Chapter Seventeen

Back in Boston, Cole chastised himself for not taking things slower with Kate. He paced the second-floor balcony overlooking the massive open concept living room, complete with a floor-to-ceiling stone fireplace and grand piano. Had he become a billionaire who'd forgotten what it was like to be poor? No, he remembered all too well.

He shoved a hand through his hair, cursing under his breath. He should have given Kate the legal documents proving she was off the hook yesterday. Why had he hesitated? He cursed again. He'd screwed things up. Worse, he didn't want her to stay because of Rosa's contract, he wanted her to stay because she wanted to. But how could she, with all the horrible things the media had said of him?

The ice king of frozen foods had no redeeming qualities. Denying the falsehoods wouldn't help, and he wouldn't admit the truth to anyone. When the board came up with the girlfriend scheme to make him more palatable to their customers, he had to go along with it.

The worst part, he didn't want a woman in his life right now, so why couldn't he stop thinking about Kate? Was Rosa, the matchmaker, that good? After all, his exec, Josh, had given Rosa his gold seal—and that meant something coming from him.

Cole shouldn't have jumped the gun and asked

Kate to continue pretending to be his girlfriend. He was already in too deep. One kiss and he'd lost his sanity, and, it seemed, his ability to be logical. He'd be better off to stay away. Cole Prentice, the billionaire, had fallen on his face. And, darn it, it hurt.

An hour later, at the office, he continued to pace. His best method to figure things out. That he hadn't worn a hole in his carpeting was a wonder. Now and then, he'd catch the expression Mrs. Evans threw his way. As if she thought he might need serious help. Come to think of it, she wasn't far from wrong.

Since she'd been with the company since his father's time, she knew more about its inner workings than he did in some ways. He smiled when he strode past the door. With any luck, it should ease any fears he'd lost his grip. Rather, she'd think he was mulling over some weighty business decision.

Except, he *was* losing his grip, and maybe one more serious than anything that could happen at Prentice. He forced himself to sit at his desk and concentrate on paperwork. He shuffled papers around but accomplished nothing. Even though he'd stared at each document for a lengthy period, he hadn't focused on a single word. His attention kept going back to his phone. Kate hadn't contacted him since he dropped her off.

He hadn't called her, either. His primary goal was to give her some space first. Some time to think, and time to forgive him for being an idiot. Coercing her to continue the pretense had been such a stupid idea. He dropped his head into his hands. But if he told her his true feelings right now, she'd have every right to want to run a mile from him.

"Cole?"

He jumped. He'd been so deep into his own misery he'd missed Josh coming into his office. "Yes?" He sat up and straightened his hair.

"Not like you to look stressed, boss." Josh took a chair.

He must've read more into Cole's expression, because he cast a serious look in Cole's direction. Cole couldn't think straight enough to back paddle the truth.

"Anything wrong, boss?"

Cole bit his lip. He considered his words. Why hadn't he been honest with Kate? Flipping a silver ballpoint pen over and over between his fingers, until he'd nearly blurted everything to Josh, he regained composure. "I received a message from the board today?" Cole threw the pen down. "Did you read the papers yesterday? In particular, the article about the pairing of frozen dinners with tantalizing dessert?"

"I did. The news article created a catchy headline. Why would the board take offense at that?"

"Oh no. They are far from offended. My relationship with the *cupcake queen* has created a worse problem. They think it's the best marketing ploy in a decade." He sighed. "And they want me to take over Kate's business. Whether friendly or hostile."

"What? Oh, hell no!" Josh sputtered. "They turned this into a takeover bid? What about your image? The beautiful woman on your arm?"

"I'm guessing they liked that idea, too, but they want the dessert more."

Josh crossed one leg over the other before planting his chin on his palm. "What should we do? Will Kate sell?"

Cole shook his head. "Even if she wanted to sell, which she doesn't, it wouldn't be to me. I can guarantee it."

"What if you found another dessert company to buy out?"

"I considered that. I even suggested it, but the board is unanimous—well, minus my vote. They want Cinnful Cupcakes introduced onto our product line as soon as possible."

"I see." Josh leaned back, one arm over the chair. "Heartless groups like them deserve what they get. Other than your obvious worries, how did your weekend go?"

"Aces." The muscles in Cole's jaw ached.

Josh's eyebrows shot up.

For most people, Cole's simple word might come across as sarcastic, but Josh and he had been friends since youth. Josh could read him.

"O.M.G. You've fallen for her, haven't you?"

Cole picked up the pen again, paying too much attention to it.

"I gather the feeling's not quite mutual?"

"Not at all mutual," Cole gritted through his teeth. "I didn't handle this situation very well, I'm afraid."

"There's a first time for everything. Even the almighty Cole Prentice can make a mistake and fall in love." Josh leaned forward. "You're allowed, Cole. You know that, don't you?"

"I make plenty. Don't you read the papers?" Bitterness broke through his words.

"Okay, man, this situation must be salvageable. You're one of the most eligible bachelors on the planet. What woman wouldn't want to align their business with yours?"

"It's not her business I want to align with. No, she'd never agree to selling to me, even if I were a trillionaire. If I ask her now, it'll seem as if it'd been my plan all along."

Josh whistled. "Man. I never expected I'd hear those words. I told you how good Rosa was."

"Yeah, she's good all right. She can even find a woman for a man who doesn't want one."

Josh smiled. "But?"

"But I've blown it, Josh. I coerced her to go along with my plan after I found out she wasn't a vetted client. I coerced her to come with me to San Francisco. Worse, I threatened both her business and Rosa's if she didn't agree."

His mouth gaped, but Josh didn't utter a word.

"I'm a jerk, I know." Cole spread his hands. "Then, when we arrived in San Francisco, things lightened up. We had fun. We enjoyed the sights and each other's company." Cole stared off into the distance. Enjoyed wasn't the word. "I don't even know how she could put aside the things I did to her long enough to—"

"To?"

"Enjoy herself." Cole's mouth tightened.

"Just how much did she enjoy herself?" Josh asked, then winked.

Cole stared at the pen. "No, we didn't—she didn't. Drat it, you know what I'm saying."

"Yeah, I didn't mean to add weight to your troubles. She seems like a nice girl from all I've read."

Cole narrowed his gaze at Josh. "You read everything?"

Josh nodded. "Everything. But I didn't believe half

of it. I investigated Rodney Hollander III, a.k.a. jerk. He's a piece of work. I'm surprised Kate ever considered marrying him. It'd be no wonder if she's man shy."

Cole exhaled. "That's why this whole thing is going south so fast. I can't do this to Kate, but I'm stuck. If I turn down the board's request right now, then they might oust me prematurely." He gritted his teeth. "You know how serious our timeline is right now. I'm nearly done, just a couple more weeks, and they can do whatever they want. It won't matter. But I need those two weeks."

Once upon a time, their business was family run. That ended when his father went off the rails. Since then, he and his mother had garnered investors because the financially crippled company made it impossible to do otherwise. He was the most invested CEO in the U.S.

"But if you agree to their request, you'll risk any chance you might have had with Kate?"

"Didn't know you were a romantic, Josh." Cole ran a hand through his ruffled mane of too-thick hair, resting a hand on the back of his neck with his head tipped forward. "Who am I kidding? No matter how interested I am, after the things I've done, there's no way she'd be interested in me."

He held up an index finger. "Don't forget your bank account has sway power, too. Maybe you can convince her, and love will come later?"

An ache in his chest spread. "Never. She's the one woman in the world who could have wanted me for me. She hates the fact that I have money."

"You're not serious…" Josh trailed off. He rubbed

his upper lip with one finger. "The best you can do right now is offer her a deal she can't turn down."

"Brilliant, why didn't I think of that? Oh wait, she wants nothing from me." Cole exhaled and adjusted his taut shoulders. He realized the company should come second, even though his mother, as well as so many long-term dedicated employees, counted on him. Truth was, he'd given up his freedom for the last fifteen years, and he was almost ready to say he'd fulfilled his promise to the employees. Two more weeks and he'd have their pensions secured.

He cast a worried glance at Josh, the only person aware he'd been working to reinstate funds stolen by his father. His mother knew a little of it, but not the full extent. He and Josh kept the volatile information from the board until they'd locked down the pension funds.

Josh stood. "Get a good night's sleep. You look tired. This will work out for you, my friend. You deserve this."

Cole pursed his lips and shook his head. "I hope you're right, Josh. At any rate, thanks for the pep talk."

"Any time, Cole." Josh looked at Cole's desk, then at his watch. "I'm guessing you're not going to escape any time soon?"

"I'll go through some of this before I leave." Cole ignored Josh's worried glance.

Josh hesitated. "Night, Cole. See you tomorrow."

"Tomorrow," Cole said automatically. He'd already opened a file, and his concentration had shifted to it. In the end, he got very little done. Kate kept interrupting his thoughts. After hours of deliberation, Cole sauntered eight blocks to Kate's apartment building.

The walk gave him time to figure out his approach. Maybe going out for dinner would be the best way to get her to listen. He passed several people jogging and exercising their dogs. Their carefree smiles ticked him off. Maybe because they appeared to have everything in control, while his world was spiralling?

He paused a few feet from Kate's door. Even though she was supposed to be on vacation. To be at his beck and call, he expected she'd have gone to work today.

With every intention to find out, he raised a hand to stab the entry buzzer.

"What are you doing here?"

He jerked around to find her watching him from the sidewalk with car keys dangling in one hand, and her purse slung over her shoulder. She wore a soft pink sleeveless top, black capris, and flip-flops. As always, she dressed in casual attire but was able to stride any runway.

When he smiled, he felt the skin on his face tighten. He noticed she didn't hide the fact that she wasn't happy to see him. She didn't buy the grin, either. Worse, he didn't have a clue how to change her mind, because he was pretty sure dinner was out of the question.

****

When Kate returned from the market and found Cole standing on her doorstep, dressed in an expensive suit and shiny leather shoes, at seven o'clock, she inhaled a long breath. Normally, he'd be all business, but tonight, his tie had been loosened, and he'd ruffled his hair beyond his normal neat self.

She scratched the back of her ear and prepared

herself for what might come next. Even though his crooked tie, and sincere expression, reminded her of the real Cole she'd seen in San Francisco, she didn't know which version stood on her doorstep—until his gaze rested on her, and his expression softened just a little. She smiled in return.

"I'm glad I caught you." He eyed her long and hard.

She noted the strain lurking behind his smile and realized his gaze had panned over her shoulder, searching for paparazzi. She followed his gaze and scanned the road, the vehicles, and even the canopy of trees lining the sidewalk. Of course, the paparazzi were there watching, but this time, she couldn't see them. She sighed and grabbed his arm. "C'mon. Let's get inside, so we won't be fodder for the press."

"Too late." He tipped his head in the general vicinity of a camera-wielding man, half hidden by a bush on the other side of the street.

She unlocked the door and let him into her apartment. Once inside, she breathed a sigh of relief. "I thought they might follow us right to the door." She leaned against the closed door. "Should I lock it? Would they try to come inside?"

He shook his head slowly, while looking around her apartment. "No. We could call the police if they did that."

She expected him to be surprised by her tiny apartment. It was far from a showcase.

His attention shifted to her, his deep brown eyes serious. "I'm sorry I've put you in this situation, Kate."

She raised a cautious eyebrow. "To tell the truth, I am also sorry. You don't deserve any of this, either."

"We need to talk."

Hearing his dire tone, she swallowed hard. As she expected, he wasn't here for a friendly visit. "Whatever it is you have to say, tell me now." She appreciated that he hadn't kissed or touched her outside for the cameras. This was a whole new level of serious for him…that scared her a lot.

Could she de-escalate his solemnity by telling him she and Rosa had visited Rosa's lawyer and found Cole's paperwork acceptable?

They were off the hook, and just like that, Rosa had forgiven him.

Cole sat in the wingback chair away from the window, then scrubbed a hand over his jaw. "I don't mean to be so typical of what you expect me to be." He sighed and looked around again. "Nice place."

Her apartment must seem like a straw hut compared to his home. She lived a meager lifestyle, putting most of her money back into her business. She enjoyed her life, though, and this small place was more than she'd ever had growing up in foster care. It gratified her when he didn't put it down. She had made it pleasing to the eye. "Tea or coffee?"

If only he'd just blurt out whatever he wanted to tell her. Had he changed his mind about the legal document? Too late if he had. According to the lawyer, the document was ironclad.

"Have you anything stronger?"

She thought about the contents of her cupboards. "I have tea and coffee and maybe some orange juice. I might have a bottle of tequila somewhere."

His eyebrows twitched. "Didn't think you'd be a tequila gal."

"I'm not," she admitted. "But Rodney was."

"Ugh. It explains so much." He flicked a piece of lint off his slacks.

"Doesn't it?" she had to grin at his remark.

"A cup of coffee would be nice."

She didn't buy it when he adjusted his pose to appear more relaxed. He was definitely tense. She brewed the coffee, added a little cream, the way he liked it, then put three cupcakes on a plate. "I don't always have cupcakes on hand, but I've been creating new recipes since I got home."

"That's why it smells heavenly in here." He grinned and ran a hand through his messy hair.

"Any chance you'd give me your opinion while you're here?" She held out the plate. "This one is double pecan chocolate, this one is strawberry cream, and this one is coconut piña colada crumble."

He regarded each one, turning them in his hand. "They all look delicious."

He took a piña colada cupcake, bit into it, and moaned. "Oh wow. I can see why your business is so popular."

Customer satisfaction always elevated her pride. She smiled. "Okay, this is a keeper. Now, take a bite of the other two, and give me your honest opinion." She had the feeling she was putting off the inevitable, but for a few moments, she enjoyed the comradery they'd managed twice in San Francisco.

He tasted the chocolate next. Then the strawberry cream. He nodded and smiled.

"They're all delicious. I would keep every one of them." He finished the piña colada while he sipped at his coffee. "How many employees do you hire?"

"I have six right now. Three for the busy morning shift, and three for later in the day and evening." She stiffened at the direction this conversation was going. Why was he asking questions about her cupcake shop? "Cole, why don't you just tell me why you're here?"

He cleared his throat. "What makes you think I'm here for anything other than a visit?"

"Maybe it's because I've learned the hard way to be cautious." She hoped her comment made him feel a little guilty. He showed no sign of it.

He sipped his coffee again.

Whatever he had to tell her, she wouldn't like it, that much she knew from his body language. "I'll get you another cup." She jumped up and took his cup before going back to the little kitchen.

"I don't have coffee in the afternoon, but I have to admit you make a tasty cup."

"C'mon, Cole. What is it?" She hated the fact she already sounded resigned to whatever bad news he was here to give her.

"Is Rosa okay with the legal agreement?"

Kate frowned. "You haven't talked to her?"

His hands fidgeted on the arm of the chair. "Not yet. I wanted to talk to you first."

She set his second cup down on the end table and sat opposite him, bracing herself.

He took another drink. "Have you ever considered selling your business?"

Instant blood drained from her face. The worm had twisted. "I'm sure you know I'd never sell my business. What are you up to?" She crossed her arms over her chest and narrowed her eyes. *Selling her cupcake enterprise. He can't be serious.*

Besides, the legal document said he wouldn't... Wait. The document said he wouldn't slander Rosa's business. It didn't say a word about taking her own business out from under her. Her legs shook, and she pressed her knees tight. "Why do you want Cinnful Cupcakes? You have a flourishing empire of frozen foods. You don't need my business, too." If he started a hostile takeover, then she'd lose. Big time. She had investors who might enjoy gaining back their investment benefits right now.

"My board thinks it'd be the feather in our proverbial cap."

She sighed. "I'm getting to the point of annoyance with you and your board. Don't billionaires get to pull their own strings?"

He pursed his lips. "As I mentioned before, extenuating circumstances dictated a financial union with other shareholders. Therefore, I must answer to the board."

"Did the board tell you to make me pretend to be your date?"

"Sort of, but I'm glad I did it."

"Wish I could say the same thing." Panicked by his news, she remained still. *She might lose her business.*

"There might be an upside to this whole thing. If you sold to my company, you'd get a bigger place. Have you considered that?"

"How much room do I need? And I'm assuming you'd want my recipes, the original ones I've created. Recipes that keep my customers coming back?"

He closed his eyes and sighed. "You could start a new business. Invent some new recipes. With the extra cash flow, with your experience and connection in the market, you'd do well."

"I'm already doing well." Her breath became shallow and quick, she couldn't get a solid breath. He could take her business out from under her because she also had investors to answer to. But why would he? She'd gone along with everything he wanted. To the point of liking him—just a little. "I've worked for years to have name recognition and market share. After perfecting my recipes, I have a unique product, a product unlike other cupcake shops. Who's saying I'll ever create something else that will work as well? Even if I wanted to—and I don't."

He removed a pad from his pocket, scribbled a number on the paper, and handed it across the table. "The board will pay you this much for your business."

She took the paper. Her hand shook. He could've just said the words out loud, but they had more impact written. All those zeros. Five million dollars. Her heart sank. They wanted her company bad enough to offer a ridiculous amount of money.

A tear escaped, and she squeezed her eyes shut. Not good at all. If she hadn't had to borrow money from Rosa, she might have reimbursed her investors with a healthy bonus within three or four years. Even though reimbursement within a few years had been the deal from the beginning, she'd gone past the promised time.

They might jump on the offer from Prentice, especially if they wanted their money and a tremendous bonus.

She blinked back tears, not making eye contact as she handed back the paper. "I want to see my business grow and succeed as much as you want to save your business. Or your image, or whatever plan you've got going." She lifted her gaze to his.

He scratched the back of his neck, while his liquid brown eyes focused on her.

Even though that look made her knees weak, she wanted to slap him. "Tell me, would you sell your business if someone offered you all the zeros you wanted?"

He let out a long breath and stared into the cup clutched in his hand. "In a heartbeat."

Not what she expected him to say. She shifted in her chair. "Is there anything else you want?" She was tired and frustrated. This version of Cole Prentice, sitting in her living room, appeared out of his element. Like a male army doll sitting in a pink doll camper. He didn't fit.

"We make a good team, Kate. We could work together."

Her heart thudded against her ribcage. If he'd said he had even the tiniest iota of feelings for her, then it might have been enough to build on. Because for some unexplainable reason she'd fallen for a man who wanted to use her in order to buy out her business, while offering her baubles to keep her appeased. She averted her gaze, swallowing hard. "No, I won't put myself in a situation like that ever again."

His eyebrows shifted. "Wait a minute, you're not comparing me to your ex, Rodney Hollander, are you?"

She shrugged. *If the shoe fits* hung in the dead air between them.

"I promise I am not like him. He was awful to you, Kate. No way am I like Hollander."

She flinched so fast she didn't have time to hide it.

"You don't know the truth. The media's version of what happened isn't true." A tear escaped and plopped onto her arm. "Please leave."

"I'm sorry." He heaved a sigh. "The board has locked onto the idea that the frozen food king is in love with his dessert queen, and they'll make the perfect amalgamation. They want to create a bigger company positioned to sell everything from breakfast to dessert."

"You can do that without my company! Wait a minute, does this mean I'm selling myself in the bargain, too?" Her hands were shaking. "No way! I can't believe I was changing my opinion of you."

Standing up, he paced to the window and gazed out.

His shoulders looked taut. Or was it because he wasn't used to being told *no*?

"I'm afraid you do not know how successful our acting was in California. Haven't you seen the news since you arrived home? We're all the media is talking about. The perfect couple who both make great food."

She shook her head. "I guess it explains the extra-long lines outside of my bakery. Maybe my female customers are hoping to get a glimpse of the handsome billionaire."

He quirked a quick smile. "You think I'm handsome?"

"Please go away and don't come back." She kept her voice as monotone as possible. This was worse than what Rodney had done. At least, he didn't steal her business. She stood, picked up his empty coffee cup, and took it to the kitchen. She turned her back. No way did she want to cry in front of him.

Her shoulders slumped after she shut the door. She

burst into tears. Not because of his betrayal, but because, beyond all reason, she cared for Cole more than she could understand.

Chapter Eighteen

Back at home, Cole couldn't get Kate's expression of utter devastation out of his mind. He understood why she didn't want to sell her business. He might as well have taken her heart and stomped on it. He didn't agree with a takeover, but he could do very little to stop the board's attempt. He was nothing but a powerless figurehead right now.

Pacing back and forth in front of his patio doors, he figured a way out of this mess. Darn it. He couldn't forgive himself if she lost everything. He'd already taken advantage of her against her will. And when he told her what was about to happen, he'd seen despair burning in the depths of her eyes. She hadn't called him the lowest, but she had every right.

She was a one-of-a-kind woman, and he'd ruined whatever chance he might have.

He'd seen the similar depth of loss in his mother's eyes when his father had betrayed her and the company. He'd fought hard to get the business back to solvency because his father had stolen all the money from the employees' pension funds. Cole worked hard to replace the funds, and with any luck, the employees would never know. Two more weeks, and with Josh's help, he'd have it all reinstated and locked in.

As if thinking about his mother conjured her up, she appeared, dressed in workout clothing with a bottle of designer water in her hand.

"Hi, Cole. Are you okay? Is something bothering you?"

"I didn't realize you were here." He turned. "Using the gym again?" *Changing the subject.*

She glanced down at her gym attire. "Yes, I'm trying a new weight training regimen. I hate attending a club. All those prying eyes. I much prefer the privacy of your gym." She tipped her head. "Again, I'll ask, why are you here, and why are you pacing? You're never home in the afternoon. Are you sick?" Her delicate brows formed tiny lines on her forehead.

"Mom, you know how hard I've worked to regain Prentice, don't you?" *That did it. Now, she appeared a notch above concerned.*

"Of course, I do. Why do you ask?"

He shoved his hands into his pockets and hunched his shoulders. "Because I'm about to do something that might ruin everything."

"Do tell?"

Cole noted she didn't sound the least bit concerned by his statement. He stopped pacing under his mother's eagle eye. "If everything goes to hell, I'm making sure the employees have ironclad protection. They will have their pensions."

She smiled, then took a sip of her water.

Had his mother been listening? "Why are you so calm about this? Are you listening?"

She touched his cheek. "I always listen, my darling. But you haven't told me what's going on yet."

"I might give up the company. Let the board take it after we wrap up the pension plan so no one else can get their hands on it."

"Good for you, dear."

He frowned. "Huh?"

She took another sip of water. "Yes, it's true. I'm happy for you because, for the first time since your father left us high and dry, you're doing something for yourself. You can't spend your whole life fixing someone else's mistakes."

"It might mean no dividends for you ever again." He spread his hands out. "I'll have to sell this place, too."

"It's too big for you, anyway." She cast a nonchalant gaze his way. "And, I'll be fine. I can rough it in a public gym." She laughed, then narrowed her hazel eyes. "Who is she?" Her eyes widened and she snapped her fingers. "Wait, it's the woman you've been dating, isn't it? The one in the limo who the media adores. She is beautiful."

Until now, he hadn't realized his mother might want to see him married. Maybe give her grandchildren. Good grief, why hadn't he contemplated it before? He ignored her question. "But without dividends, how will you manage?"

She eyed her manicured nails, painted an opalescent pink. "You don't have to worry about me. I'm the Prentice in the family, not your father. I have funds never connected to the company. We might have to change the *B in billionaire to an M*, but we'll get by just fine."

"But you put every cent into the business?"

"One thing your grandfather taught me long ago, Cole, was how to diversify. Never put all your money in one investment, and never risk another investment in a failing enterprise."

"Wow." A wave of relief washed over him. "I guess I should have asked you about your financial situation. To be honest, I've done the same thing to a small degree. I'm a silent partner in a start-up business that is doing well."

"I didn't think you'd listened when I'd told you not to put everything into one portfolio. I'm so glad to hear you have other investments not connected to Prentice." She grimaced. "Your father created a heck of a mess for you to sort out. I can't tell you how proud I am to know you're securing our employees' pensions, but I'm not sure why you have to?"

"I couldn't let our loyal employees pay for Father's betrayal. He took the pensions and gambled the money away. It would be the stain on our name, and your name, if their pensions disappeared." His knuckles ached from fisting them so hard. "So far, no one else knows but Josh and me."

Victoria took his hand and squeezed. "I was afraid he might have tampered with the pensions. I just wasn't sure. You also had to do this to get your father's betrayal out of your system. I know you. If you hadn't saved the company for the employees, it would have weighed on you."

"That's true." He wrapped an arm around her shoulders.

"If you'd confided in me, then I would have helped sooner. Thing is, I didn't think it necessary—you seemed to take running the business in stride."

"I didn't need help. And, I wouldn't have allowed you to pour more money into Prentice. The employees are now protected. I must finalize a couple more documents to shore everything up. By the end of next week, I'll get out from under the threat. Hopefully, the truth will never come out."

"After you're gone, what do you think will happen to Prentice?"

"With a group of investors who only care about the money, I imagine our product will suffer. They're not very interested in quality." He pursed his mouth.

"It's so bad? I didn't realize." She shook her head. "That said, it's time to let it go, son."

Cole inhaled. "I can't believe how many things have changed in a week. My personal priorities take precedence now."

She patted his cheek. "I'm proud of you, and so happy to hear you're doing the right thing—at last."

"But the Prentice name…"

She cleared her throat, then took another slow sip of water. "Do you think the name means anything if we aren't true to ourselves?"

He didn't understand. "Wasn't that what Dad had been—true to himself? And he almost ruined the company in his selfish wake."

"Now, hold on." Both hands rose in front of her. "Your father might have been selfish, and he might have come close to bankrupting Prentice, but don't you think somewhere deep down he had reasons for doing what he did? He has an illness, yes. I hate to say this and destroy the image you have of your grandfather, but he put too much store in money—and favorites. Your grandfather neglected your father. Treated him like an ingrate who deserved nothing, including love. When we married, your father tried so hard to measure up to your grandfather's expectations. He believed if he had a rich wife and a child, he'd proved his worth." Her eyes glassed over, and her bottom lip trembled.

"Mom, I'm sorry. You don't have to…"

"When he realized he'd failed us, too, it crippled him. He gave up, and it was the end of the man I'd fallen in love with. After that, he got trapped in the downward spiral, putting him where he is today. Since he never gained the love and understanding from his father, he'd lost his ability to interact with everyone. With me."

"And now he's an ex-addict in a group home." Cole gritted his teeth, attempting to control deep-seated anger at his father's weakness. He wanted to have sympathy for the man who'd left them and who'd stolen and gambled away a lion's share of the company's money, who'd lied to the media, and had made his son a pariah in his own community to save his own skin. All his father's efforts were to make himself appear more sympathetic, while throwing Cole under the bus, as if Cole had been the one who'd mismanaged the money.

"Someday you'll understand and be able to forgive your father. He needs your forgiveness more than you know. But never mind that now. I think you have more uplifting things going on in your life." She nodded her assurance.

"It's true. I've realized what's more important. I've had an epiphany of sorts."

His mother smiled. "You've fallen in love."

His gut twisted. He didn't disagree. How could he? "I don't understand it. I've just known her for a week, Mom. I hired her from a matchmaking company."

"Well, that's not what I expected to hear." Victoria laughed.

"She hates me."

"Are you sure?" Victoria's voice escalated, and her brows rose. "Being a billionaire doesn't impress her? She still doesn't want you?"

"Correct." She seemed even more interested. His teeth glued together.

"You mean she's beautiful, in a down-to-earth, not a stuck-up socialite kind of way?" Victoria Prentice raised her brows.

"You've been reading the papers, I take it," Cole replied.

"Of course, my darling. But if you ask me, she seemed very interested in you."

Cole stiffened. "Staged photos for the press. I'm afraid I blackmailed her into going along with the charade. I told her I'd ruin the matchmaker's business, owned by her friend, and maybe her own business."

Mom planted her hands on her hips. "Oh, Cole, you didn't. It doesn't sound like you at all."

He sighed. "I had to; otherwise, she would have left me high and dry."

Victoria laughed. "I'm liking the sound of this girl more and more. She doesn't care about your wealth. She sounds like the right woman for you, son. It says something about her character. Not to mention, you care for her, and it's been just a few days since you met her."

"Yes, just a few days." His mother was right. It seemed as if he'd known Kate longer—forever—and he wanted more, much more. "But I'm afraid I'll never convince her I'm not the jerk I projected from the start. I didn't know the board would see the news articles and decide we'd make a good team, as in amalgamation in business and in romance. If she doesn't agree, then they're willing to take Kate's cupcake enterprise, either with consent or through a hostile takeover."

"Oh, no, that's awful." Victoria frowned.

"Doesn't matter, I'm not doing it. I'm meeting with the board in two hours. At which time, they'll oust me as the board director, and my position as president will go a short time after. They won't be able to force me out before the pension funds are solid, though. I've made sure."

His mother wiped a tear from the corner of her eye. "I've never been prouder, Cole. If you take a survey of the Prentice family history, I don't think many of them were happy, if any. They were too busy making more money. It's time to break the mold."

"I'm surprised to hear you say that, Mom." He screwed up his face. "You're willing to wipe away everything your family has done in the last four generations?"

"I changed the company to your father's last name after we were married. Since I'd already wiped away generations of family name. No one cared, not as long as the money kept coming in."

"Why did you do that?"

"It seemed it might help your father prove to the world he was worthy. Prove to himself he was worthy." She sighed.

"I'm sorry it didn't work, Mom."

"No, the damage had been done, and he couldn't overcome it." She smiled, but a tear plopped onto her cheek. "It seems you're like me, my darling son. You know what's important, and you can let the company go if the employees are secure. I'm very proud of you."

"You don't care?"

"Not at all. And, even better, if it means you'll have a wonderful life with the perfect woman." She wrapped her arms around him in a gentle hug.

"Thanks, Mom." He grinned. "It means a lot to me to know I have your approval."

"And you mean a lot to me. Go get her!"

Cole's heart tightened. *Hopefully, Kate felt the same way about him.*

Chapter Nineteen

In Kate's wonderful bakery—her happy place—she distracted herself by making her favorite signature cupcakes. Thanks to her grandmother's secret recipe, the chocolate icing tasted like fudgy heaven. She believed Granny's special recipe had helped to make her business a success.

Kate gazed at her shop. She'd decorated with a red-and-white sixties theme, with booths, round tables with seats, and stools covered with red vinyl. She'd even found old music boxes for the booths linked to the jukebox in the corner. Two records out of ten were stuck, but her customers loved the old tunes. The glass cases, hosting cupcakes and pastries, had been vintage, as well, giving her shop the ability to match her décor. Her employees wore tiny red aprons with white ruffles to complete the theme. Behind the counter was a half wall, so she could see her customers from the back.

The decadent vanilla-bean cupcakes topped with fudge-swirl icing never lasted long. A line waited outside her shop every Tuesday, *Decadent Cupcake Day*. Today was no different. Well, maybe a little different. Because of the recent media coverage, the line was even longer this morning. "We'd better pack these into boxes of six." Kate handed Dierdre a case of boxes. "We already have a long line, and we don't open for another twenty minutes."

"Already on it, boss." Dierdre hefted the packages. "We can save these until tomorrow. I put the boxes together an hour ago, while you were icing the cupcakes."

Kate appreciated that she had all the cupcakes tucked into their boxes within the time she'd washed the dishes, then put them away—five minutes before they opened for the day.

"You're always a step ahead of me, Dee." Kate checked her watch. "Are we ready for the rush?"

Dierdre took a long swig of her water. "All hydrated and ready to go." She grinned.

Wiping her hands over her signature apron, Kate smiled at her patrons as she unlocked and opened the door.

How long could she hold on to her business if Prentice continued with a takeover bid? Kate's happiness soured, and she glanced at Dierdre, who was unaware of possible unemployment in her future. Kate needed a miracle.

After lunch, and making sure the rush was over, Kate called Rosa to ask if they could meet for coffee. Twenty minutes later, she stepped into a cafe nearest her bakery and chose a table in the corner. She'd just ordered two coffees when Rosa arrived.

"I'm so sorry, Kate. I thought the media had been unfair to Cole. Now, he's poised to take over your business." Rosa stirred sugar into her cup. "It's my fault you're in this mess. What if I pay out the investors and their bonuses? Then Cole's company can't take over, because the business will be yours again?"

Kate smiled, but her insides were acid. "Neither of us can afford that right now, but I appreciate the offer.

Besides, I put myself in this mess, Rosa. You might have asked me to date Cole, but I accepted, and my actions alone started this takeover bid. It's my fault, not yours."

"Why do you think that?" Rosa's voice lowered.

"I guess my acting was too good." She forced a light tone but failed. "Cole told me his board liked the public relations aspect, and they think it'll make for great marketing if they add my cupcakes to their frozen food lineup."

Rosa's eyes narrowed, and she leaned toward her friend. "No. We adore your pastries *fresh*. People don't want to buy them frozen. Wait a minute. What else aren't you telling me?"

She couldn't keep a secret from Rosa. She needed some words of wisdom right now. "I think I love him." *There, she'd blurted it out.* Maybe now she could have a good cry when she went home.

Rosa flew back in her chair and covered her mouth—not doing an excellent job at hiding the huge smile. "Wait, another darned minute. You said you'd never let yourself love again, not with someone like Cole Prentice."

Kate swallowed a hard lump that threatened to force hot tears. "I know. I can't understand it, but now I must get past it. Of course, his feelings aren't mutual. How could I have let this happen, Rosa?"

Rosa took a gulp of her coffee before her fingers started tapping on the table. She was quiet for a couple of minutes. "I have the feeling it'll all work out." She smiled.

"That's your advice?"

"For now. Knock me over with a feather. I had an

inkling about you two, even though deep down I wasn't sure, especially after he threatened us. But, if you are in love with Cole Prentice, it proves my abilities as a matchmaker, because I had thought so from the start."

Kate frowned at Rosa. "While you gloat over the proof of your abilities, don't forget who the victims are here. My feelings are one-sided. I'm just a means to an end for Cole. A rental girlfriend for the media. Now it's over, and I won't see him again. With Prentice enacting a hostile takeover bid of my bakery, I don't know what to do." She pressed fingers against her forehead, as if that could calm her nerves.

Rosa's eyebrows shot up, and her hand gripped Kate's on the table. "I don't understand. Is Cole behind the takeover? I know he's a cold-hearted business exec according to the media, but would he do this to you, after everything you did to help him? Besides, you'd never fall for someone fake."

"Really?" Kate grimaced. "Have you forgotten Rodney?"

"He doesn't count. He got what he deserved, marrying a spoiled-rotten daddy's girl with little-to-no-brains."

"I don't think she's so bad." Kate sighed. "I see her as a victim, too."

"Never mind that. How did you find out about the impending takeover?"

"Cole told me." Kate wrung her hands on her lap.

"See." Rosa reached out and touched Kate's arm. "He cares about you. Otherwise, why would he let you know what the board was doing? Plus, you two had some chemistry in San Francisco, no?"

"I admit he's a great kisser. It was hard pretending

to be in love in front of the paparazzi. I had to keep reminding myself it wasn't real, because sometimes, I believed it. Maybe I have the syndrome people get when kidnapped?"

Rosa laughed. "Stockholm syndrome? That'd be iffy, considering you weren't kidnapped."

"I shouldn't have fallen for him, though. I should know better." She covered her eyes with her hands. "I'm doomed to fail in the love department."

"Are you sure your feelings aren't mutual? I mean, how can he not fall for you? You're beautiful, smart, and you can do anything you set your mind to."

Kate blew out a breath. "No, he couldn't even look me in the eye when he told me about the looming hostile takeover."

"But that's different. Didn't you say the board is telling him what to do these days? He doesn't have control of his own company anymore. It must be awful to lose control of your family's company. And, don't forget, he gave you notice so you could figure out what you need to do to save your company."

"I suppose." Kate's chest lightened.

"And what, if anything, did he tell you about needing a relationship at the beginning?"

"Although he was straightforward about what he wanted, when he found out you and I were friends, he said he didn't want an actual relationship, just a part-time girlfriend to get the media off his back."

Rosa cleared her throat. "I know I'm being personal, but did he coerce you into bed?"

Kate pursed her lips and remembered that evening. "No. He didn't try—not really." She let out a long, wavering sigh. "Not sure what would have happened if he had." Her face flushed.

Rosa clapped her hands together. "I'll fix this, somehow, Kate. I'll talk to my lawyer right away to see if Cole's company's attempt to take over your business is a violation of our matchmaking contract. We could construe it to be the reason he hired you, and that would be a breach of promise."

"But he didn't find out about the takeover bid until we returned home."

"If he told you the truth." Rosa winked. "I know you care, but if he's under the thumb of the board, he might not even care if we play that card."

"Oh, I don't know. I'm so worried right now. Thanks for trying to help. If you think we can go after the company for breach, let me know. Either way, I'll have to get my investors together, including you, to see if they'll stay with me, or if they intend to go with the quick return on their money."

"Right. Sounds like a good plan. Just let me know when you're holding the meeting. I'll be there."

Kate drained her cup. "I must return to work. Thanks for your advice and for always being my friend."

"Don't be silly, Kate. You and I are peas in a pod—*compadres*."

"Guess that's true. I didn't expect to tell you about my true feelings, even though we're best friends. I'm not sure I had even figured it out for myself before I blurted it out." She raised her hands. "What is wrong with me? Why do I always fall for the wrong men?"

"You don't—at least, not anymore. Besides, this will work out—I might have to put out a psychic Rosa shingle before we're done." Rosa winked, picked up her purse, and snatched her cellphone out. "I have a few calls to make, dear. Try not to worry. I'll call you later." She exited the cafe, already talking.

Kate picked up her purse, then followed Rosa out. She paused at the corner, inhaling several times to quell her rising anxiety. How would it all work out? She was in love with a man who didn't love her back. A man who could very well drive her back to the poverty line. How had she allowed this to happen?

And, with big money backing Prentice, they could thrill her investors by buying them out with much more money than she could ever provide. They would never get her signature cupcake recipe. Nor would they get the other personal recipes she'd created by trial and error over the years. Those recipes had been the reason for her success. They were part of her limited family history and her own creations. Even though she'd been in the foster system after her parents died in a car accident, she'd kept a recipe book from her grandmother, a woman she couldn't remember. The frosting recipe she'd found inside—No way could she allow that recipe to be taken along with her business. Her stomach clenched.

Back at the shop, the line had dwindled to a dozen people, and Dierdre was ringing up orders.

The minute Kate stepped inside, Dierdre moved her eyes to the right twice. Kate turned her head.

Cole Prentice sat at one of the charming retro table and chair sets, with a box of trademark cupcakes in front of him.

Noooo!

He stood.

She waved him back down and hurried over before

anyone noticed the frozen king was in her establishment. "Why are you here?" She sat opposite him. Why had he bought her signature cupcakes? Was he taking them to the board? Proving how good they are, and making sure they'd be part of the buyout?

"I'm delivering these papers for your signature." He reached down to open a briefcase next to his leg.

Her heart pinched. Tears threatened, and as hard as she tried to hold them back, one slipped out. "How could you be so mean? So cold? I've tried to help you, and now you'll ruin me?"

His mouth thinned, and his brow furrowed. "Please read the document. I am giving you my guarantee I will not allow Prentice to take over your business. This document is the offer I'll give your investors in order to return your company to you, and to you, alone."

Flexing her tense shoulders, she glanced at the paperwork laid on the table and froze at the dollar figure he proposed for her seven investors. "They'll never be able to turn this down." More tears boiled to the surface and slid like molten caramel down her cheeks, burning a path to her chin.

"No, Kate. You don't understand."

She slouched in the chair, wiping her tears with a napkin, while he attempted to hold her other hand.

"Let me go!" She pulled back.

"Please, Kate. I will not take your business. I'm making sure your investors get their money. The business with be one hundred percent yours again and not susceptible to a takeover. I'm ensuring no one can steal it out from under you, not even Prentice."

She gritted her teeth. "Meanwhile, you'll own my business, so I'll owe you instead. How could you do this to me?" She jumped to her feet, not looking at him again before rushing to the back of her shop, a waterfall of hot tears spilling in front of her customers. Kate heard Dierdre's raised voice behind her.

"I'm sorry, sir, but you can't go back there. No customers allowed by order of the health inspector." She was very firm and didn't allow him past the counter.

That evening, Kate received a courier package from Prentice. She thought it strange Cole would send a new offer via courier. Maybe since she'd rejected his private offer, this was another tack.

She'd rather lose everything than owe Cole thousands of dollars she couldn't repay. No way. If they took her company, then she could start again—but not without her grandmother's secret icing recipe. The one she'd sworn never to share.

She flipped through the document. Page six of the takeover bid stated in bold letters her recipes must come with the business. Her chest burned. She nearly doubled over with nausea—could they make her share the recipes? She checked her watch. At twelve o'clock, it was too late to call anyone. She had no choice but to wait until morning—but, the wait would be interminable.

She spent half the night figuring out her next plan. By the next morning, she'd decided what to do. She called a hotel, booked a conference room, then phoned each investor in person, and asked if they could meet tonight for an urgent update on the business.

Her investors were available, every single one. She had the feeling it might have something to do with curiosity about her and the handsome billionaire. Could her investors afford to go along with her plan?

She didn't have to be a genius to imagine how things might go. Everyone who'd invested was a friend, or friends of friends. If even one person wanted the payout, her offer wouldn't work.

Arriving at the conference room well before anyone else, she repositioned the tables and chairs in a round-table format. Next, she placed their current investment portfolios on the tables, then poured herself a cup of strong coffee. She'd appeal to them to hang in. To have faith, because in time, she would make their investments worthwhile.

She'd planned with the hotel manager for tea and coffee to be served. The manager allowed her to use her own products as the snacks. She placed cookies and mini cupcakes on the table next to the drinks. She prayed the night would go well.

Dressed in a business-formal black suit with a colorful cupcake pin on her lapel, she wore little makeup, especially mascara, just in case she started crying again. Waiting for everyone to arrive, she crossed one leg over the other, her foot bouncing.

"Excuse me."

She must've been in a world of her own, because she jumped when an older woman stood inside the door. Not one of her investors. "I'm sorry, this is a private meeting." Kate pointed at the signage near the door. "I think you have the wrong room."

"I'm in the right place, dear. I'm Victoria Prentice." She crossed the room, taking Kate's hand in hers. "Cole's mother."

Kate stood and shook Victoria's hand, noting Cole had her eyes, very kind eyes. She appeared much too young to be his mother.

When she saw Mrs. Prentice held papers in her left hand, Kate rubbed the goose bumps forming on her arms while her back stiffened. Cole was using his mother as a go-between. Dirty pool. "I'm sorry, Mrs. Prentice, I've already told Cole I want nothing to do with his business deal. You understand, I don't want to owe anyone. I've built this business myself, and rather than answer to anyone else, I'll let it go to Prentice. It'll save Cole quite a few dollars, too."

"May I sit?" Victoria eased a chair out, then indicated for Kate to sit next to her. Victoria rattled the papers. "My dear, have you read this document through?"

Kate stared at the floor. "No. I didn't need to. I don't want to owe Cole."

"I think you should read it. Cole will pay your investors off and give them a healthy bonus. All this money is coming from him and not from the company. He's signing off on any consequence to you. You won't owe him a cent. The business will be yours, free and clear after the investors take their settlement. Cole will not bother you again." She hesitated. "If that's what you want."

Blinking hard, she glanced away when Victoria's sympathetic gaze washed over her. Kate remembered very little of her own mother. How wonderful to have someone like this woman in Cole's life. Mrs. Prentice wasn't what Kate would expect of a billionairess, either. She seemed down-to-earth.

Victoria took a slow breath before speaking again. "Kate, I'd appreciate it if you would keep what I'm about to say to yourself. We don't share this information with most people. My son took over Prentice after his father all but ran it into the ground. Cole has done nothing but work, live, and breathe Prentice for the past fifteen years—even though I've tried to convince him not to."

"Why didn't you want him to?" Kate asked.

Victoria sighed. "I didn't want my son to pay for the sins of his father. I couldn't convince him to leave and forget about the past. Good thing he didn't listen because, through his investigation into his father's ravaging of the company funds, he found out his father embezzled the pension plan of our two hundred employees." Her eyes grew watery. "Through hard work, Cole has made the business solvent again, but the board owns more of the company than we do now, thanks to Herbert, my ex-husband."

She took a tissue out of her purse and dabbed her eyes. "I'm here to give you the contracts, again, Kate, and I hope you'll reconsider Cole's offer. But I'm also here to thank you. Because of you, Cole has seen how destructive the company has become for him and for me. Life is too fleeting to put Prentice ahead of his own happiness." She touched Kate's hand. "You've helped him to see what's important. You gave him the will to sell his shares off and to let the board do whatever they want with the company, now that he's replaced the pension funds."

Turning to take Victoria in, Kate tipped her head. "How did I help him see that? I don't understand."

"My dear, he sees Prentice was someone else's dream, his great-great-grandfather's, not his. He knows his life is more important than working twenty-four-seven, thanks to you." Victoria stood and held out a hand. "I'm happy to meet you, Kate. I hope we see each other again." She laid the papers on the table.

An unwanted tear slid down Kate's cheek. She couldn't let Cole pay off her investors. To owe him money and not be able to see him would be untenable. If he allowed his mother to tell her, he must not want to see her again. A dull pain tightened in her chest. "I can't let him do this!" She watched Victoria stroll toward the doorway.

Victoria stopped near the entrance, her expression softened. "Why not, dear?"

"I don't understand why he'd do this?" Kate steadied herself by leaning on the table.

"Don't you, dear?" Victoria asked, leaving silent whatever answer might follow.

"No."

Victoria nodded. "You'll figure it out." She smiled as she left.

Kate closed her eyes and inhaled. When she made mistakes, they were epic. She should never have agreed date Cole Prentice. Her life had been going as she'd hoped. Her business was growing, and things were looking up. She didn't blame Rosa. Rosa didn't ask her to fall in love with the man who'd threatened to blackmail them. Her insides tightened.

Hearing voices in the lobby, she hurried her fingers across her hair and forced herself to smile at each person, as if the world was hers to control.

Most of them had wandered in, chatting amongst themselves. Two people still hadn't arrived.

Cole stepped into the room.

She froze.

Could she take any more pain today? Her first

instinct was to be the one who rejected him first. She rushed toward him before he made it too far inside the room. She clenched her jaw, and her teeth felt glued together. "You should leave, Cole. I won't become indebted to you, no matter how genuine your offer." She wanted to point a finger at him, but her hands were shaking. "And *way-to-use-dirty-pool*. Sending your mother to talk me into signing."

"My mother was here?" His eyes widened. "When? Why?"

Kate held up the package of contracts she'd left for the investors. She narrowed her eyebrows. "Because she delivered these."

He frowned. "What the... How'd she find those papers? How'd she even know about your meeting tonight?"

"Do you want me to believe you didn't send your mother to sweet-talk me into the deal?" she whispered, but too late, realized their furtive whispering had garnered interest from her investors.

Everyone was watching them.

With a hand spread on Cole's chest, she urged him into the hall.

But he wouldn't budge. "Yes." He used his best straightforward voice. "I did not know she'd come here. I didn't even tell her about my offer." Suspicion crossed his face. "Josh!"

"Who?"

Cole straightened his shoulders. "My vice-president, Josh Bremmer, thinks I need help to get this thing straightened out. He's called in the big gun—my mother." His mouth thinned. "He might have gone too far this time."

"It's all too much right now. I can handle my own affairs." She snatched a quick glance at the crowd. "Please leave."

"Kate." He moved toward her.

She backed away until a table stopped her retreat.

He hesitated for a second, his face impassible, but his brown eyes seemed pained.

"I'm not Rodney Hollander, Kate. I'll never let you down. If you never want to see me again, I promise I'll go away. But we need to talk first. I don't want Prentice to steal your business away. This is the best thing I can do to save you."

She put her hands up to stop him. "I don't need you to save me. I can save myself. It's something I've been doing my whole life." She hated he saw her hands shaking. "Your mother told me you'd stay away if I wanted." Her teeth clenched harder. *Why couldn't he just leave? Even though her heart ached to see him again, he'd never want her; she was way out of his league.*

"I guess she knows me too well." He held his hands out, palms up. "You have every reason to hate me, Kate. When I hired you for the job, I shouldn't have treated you like an employee. The thing is, from experiences with women, I assumed I'd be shoving you away the whole time we faked our relationship."

Kate stiffened, readying herself to tell him off.

He grimaced. "Wait, what I'm saying is, most women in my social circle, in my experience, can see nothing but the dollar signs. I'd given up ever thinking it would be possible to find someone to love, someone who'd love me for who I am, and not the size of my bank account."

She blinked, not at all what she'd expected him to say. Was he telling her he loved her? Was it even possible? "But you're offering to buy out my business. Don't you see? It means I'll owe you. If you're saying you care for me, that's no way to build a relationship."

He stepped closer.

She could smell his subtle, enticing spiced cologne and see the muscle working in his jaw. His sensual gaze weakened her resolve, making her skin heat and her knees weaken. Not a sound interrupted them.

"I meant it as a thank-you for rescuing me from a life locked to Prentice. My mother has tried for years to get me to give it up. Until a few days ago, she didn't realize I had to recoup the employees' pension investments. My father had stolen them. But now I've reimbursed the funds, and I made sure no one else can get their hands on the pensions, except the pensioners."

"I don't understand why you're telling me this?" Kate backed up until her legs hit the table. She had nowhere else to go. "Your mother told me the same thing."

His eyes widened. "She did? She never speaks of family problems to anyone. Even to me."

"She asked me to keep it to myself."

"I'm sure she did. She's still protecting my father, even though she and I were nothing but an afterthought."

Kate glanced at her investors. Every face pointed their way. She didn't think Cole's admission had been loud enough to be heard.

"You made me see I can have a life of my own. I can find someone to love. Live my life from now on."

Against the table, she placed both hands down on

either side to keep herself upright. She held her breath, didn't dare to speak in case she'd imagined his words. He loved her?

Dare she hope it was true? He hadn't said the actual words, and she'd never jump to such a reckless conclusion. No way she'd make a fool of herself by admitting she loved him, too.

It couldn't be true. She forced a calm demeanor and straightened. "No. I'm sorry. I can't accept your offer." She squeezed her hands together in front of her. "The business remains mine, and my investors will just have to wait until I've grown big enough to make their buyout appreciable. I don't know why you'd even think about paying off my investors with no strings."

He tipped his head to one side.

His gaze softened. "Can't you understand why, Kate? I thought I just made it clear. I love you, and I think you love me, too."

Kate's heart lurched, and she straightened her back—he'd said the words. "Why? I've been nothing but hard to get along with. Why would you love me?"

He smiled. "Why wouldn't I love you?"

Her heartbeat thumped in her chest.

"You're everything I've always wanted. You had my heart from the moment you stepped into my office, glared at me, and didn't back down. There's something special about you. Not to mention every time I see you, my blood pressure..." He made a motion with his thumb, showing an upward motion.

Glad she'd braced herself against the table, since her legs felt less than solid. Somewhere, in the back of her mind, his words were too good to be true. She shouldn't fall for it. He didn't know she loved him, so why would he be so cruel to say he loved her? "No, I'm sorry. You must be mistaken. You don't care for me."

He expelled a quick breath. "Why do you think that?"

"You've read the media about me. I'm a gold digger, remember?" She tasted bitterness on her tongue.

His arms crossed over his chest. "And you've read the media about me. Do you believe I'm so heartless I'd throw my father onto the street?"

"Of course not." She rubbed her forehead. "But you need to know I grew up in a rundown trailer with foster parents who were poor and not very loving. I had to work hard to pay my way through university. I'm not the girl someone like you takes home to your mother."

His brows drew together. "That's Rodney talking, isn't it? He's a heartless fool. No one worth their salt cares about that."

"Some people do." Her voice hitched against her will. Not because she cared about Rodney or pedigree, but because she cared about Cole, and she didn't want him to reject her.

His arms opened, and he waited. "Come here and prove you don't love me."

She admired his casual attire, the new haircut, neat and trim, while his smooth, shaven face and the familiar odor of soap sent her senses tingling. "No."

"Why, you afraid you might love me back, and you're afraid you'll give yourself away?"

"Of course not." She crossed her arms over her chest. "Rosa told you how I feel about rich men. I don't trust them. I don't trust you."

"I know you don't believe that. I'm not Rodney Hollander." His voice softened. "I'll never leave you in the lurch and holding the bill. Hell, I didn't even think I'd ever find someone who could love me for me, and not my money. I'd give every cent away if it would make you happy."

She blinked. "You're not serious." She hadn't shifted an inch, because she didn't trust her feet to carry her.

"Oh, yes, I am." He closed in, his breath fanned her forehead. His arms wrapped around her, and his chin rested on her head. "Doesn't this feel right?"

Oh heavens, yes. She inhaled his scent and, in an instant, forgot about the audience they had. "Maybe."

"Listen, you convinced me to start anew. Can't you do the same for me? I promise I won't let you down. After I leave Prentice, I won't be a billionaire anymore. Do you need a server in your bakery? I'm a trained barista."

She tilted her head back, eyebrows raised in his general direction.

"Just kidding, I can learn." He grinned. "But I tricked you into turning your head up just enough to…" He leaned down and planted his lips on hers.

Good thing he was holding her tight, because she couldn't stand on her own right now.

"Say it." His teeth grated against her bottom lip.

"You don't understand the depth of my fear." Her breath shuddered.

"Be honest and tell me if you think I'd do any of those things Hollander did to you, my love. I've already left Prentice, thanks to you. I'd give up everything and start over with you. Would Rodney have ever given up his status, let alone his money?"

Heat rushed through her. She believed him because

she'd fallen in love the moment he stood up to Rodney in San Francisco. Never a snob about money, she wanted to achieve her own success without his help.

Their lips met, and heat coursed through her until she thought she'd melt. *Good thing his arms were holding her as if he never wanted to let her go.*

Applause sounded in the background.

A tear slid down her face. "I do love you, and I think your mother is wonderful, too. And I can support you if you need help."

He laughed. "Of course, you love my mother. She's fantastic. It's no surprise you got along. And I don't need your help with money, my darling. I have other investments that are looking optimistic."

Legs too weak to hold her, she leaned against him, squashing her face into his chest. "Okay, just so you know, I'm still turning down your offer." She wanted everything out on the table. She looked up.

His face paled, and he leaned back to see her face. "What?"

"I'm turning down your offer to pay off my investors, because I want to manage my business without help. My investors will stay. They're my friends, as well as investors, and I think they'll stay invested in Cinnful Cupcakes for the time being."

"I'm sure you're right. You make people want to stick with you. But what about my other offer?"

"Your offer?"

"Will you marry me?"

Could it be his hands holding hers were shaking? "You're serious?" She stepped out of his arms to gauge his expression.

He nodded. "I should have been more prepared for

this. I can't get down on one knee, because I haven't had time to buy a ring." His mouth quirked downward.

"What? I…" Tears fell down her cheeks. *Could this really be true?*

"Say yes, Kate. I can't lose you." He inhaled and planted his lips on hers again.

The kiss rocked her to the core and she lost all grasp of location and time until applause brought her back to reality. All of her investors were standing and clapping.

Was this real or had it been an act? She looked around, and no paparazzi were in sight. Real this time, not fake. "I'm not sure…"

"Kate, look at me. This is the real me. You're the only woman who has ever seen me for who I am. What we've had together, it can't have all been a lie." His voice cracked.

She stared but didn't answer.

He backed away, his face unreadable.

Kate's heart lurched. "No, wait. I just needed a minute to think this through. To adjust to the idea that you love me as much as I love you. It's like a dream."

"You love me?" His eyes closed momentarily, then his smile grew. "Oh geez, don't scare me." His mouth pressed against hers again.

He kissed her with such heart, she melted into him. The memory surfaced of them waltzing on the deck, with ocean music playing in the background, and how they'd fit together.

From behind them, Rosa cleared her throat, while raising one eyebrow in their direction and clapped her hands. "I was right about you two, after all."

"Are you saying you set this up on purpose? You

were aware we'd be a match all along?" Kate turned and focused her surprise on Rosa.

Rosa winked. "Yes, from the moment I met Cole, I had the feeling he'd be your perfect match, although it was a rocky road to get you both to that conclusion."

Cole winked at Kate, then took her hand in his, and kissed the back.

Pressing her other hand against her heart, Kate inhaled. For the first time, she was loved by someone who would always have her back—a man who didn't care about money over love.

She pressed against him and lifted her face.

Being accepted and being loved was all she needed—the truth was in his kiss.

Praise for Lina Gardner

"THE BAKER AND THE BILLIONAIRE is a deliciously irresistible tale that will leave fans of opposites-attract and fake relationship tropes swooning from start to finish. Packed with sizzling chemistry, heartfelt moments, and just the right dash of drama under the media's watchful eye, this story has all the ingredients for the perfect romance. Sweet, captivating, and utterly delightful—this is the love story you'll want to devour in one sitting!"

~5 Stars, Cathryn Fox, NYT's Bestselling Author

~*~

"Lina Gardiner's THE BAKER AND THE BILLIONAIRE is a delight! Tuck in with this warm, romantic, fun story. You won't be disappointed."

~Carla Neggers, New York Times Bestselling Author

~*~

"THE BAKER AND THE BILLIONAIRE is a good romantic story with emotional depth. It will appeal to readers who enjoy romance, character-driven plots, and personal growth in characters. The characters' chemistry was very well written. Cole is a hotty!

~Betty Brousseau

~*~

"Chemistry charged with heat and volatility from beginning to end."

~Pat Gardiner

~*~

"Loved the way the characters met and the way it went from don't like you to I love you."

~Lillian Waite

A word about the author...

Lina Gardiner is an award-winning author who has won RWA-Kiss of Death's Daphne DuMaurier Award for Excellence in the Paranormal-Time Travel-Futuristic category, RT Book Reviews Reviewers' Choice Best Book Awards finalist, Kansas City, winner of the Prism Award, Best First Book, from FF&P (Futuristic, Fantasy and Paranormal Chapter of RWA), and a nominee for the Paranormal Romance Guild Reviewers' Choice Awards.

Her books have been well received by such reviewers as Kirkus Reviews and USA Today's HEA blog, including a 4.5-star rating from RT Book Reviews and nomination for Romantic Times Reviewer's Choice 2013

On the home front, Lina Lives in New Brunswick, Canada, a hot spot for legendary ghosts, tall tales and odd happenings, which probably add to her love of a good mystery. The spooky stories her grandfather told his grandchildren in the "parlor" when their grandmother wasn't paying attention also sparked the wonders of imagination and a love of storytelling.

www.linagardiner.com

Thank you for purchasing
this publication of The Wild Rose Press, Inc.

For questions or more information
contact us at
info@thewildrosepress.com.

The Wild Rose Press, Inc.
www.thewildrosepress.com